Evelyn Everett-Green

Torwood's Trust

A Novel: Vol. II.

Evelyn Everett-Green

Torwood's Trust
A Novel: Vol. II.

ISBN/EAN: 9783337065348

Printed in Europe, USA, Canada, Australia, Japan

Cover: Foto ©Andreas Hilbeck / pixelio.de

More available books at **www.hansebooks.com**

TORWOOD'S TRUST.

A Novel.

BY

EVELYN EVERETT-GREEN.

'Out of this nettle, danger, we pluck this flower,
safety . . . . I protest, our plot is as good a plot as
ever was laid.'

HENRY IV., *Pt. I., Act II., Sc. III.*

IN THREE VOLUMES.

VOL. II.

LONDON:

RICHARD BENTLEY AND SON,

Publishers in Ordinary to Her Majesty the Queen.

1884.

[*All Rights Reserved.*]

CONTENTS OF VOL. II.

TORWOOD'S TRUST.

CHAPTER I.

A SECOND ALFRED BELASSIS.

MISS MARJORY'S carefully planned dinner was a marked success, and was followed by a very pleasant evening, spent partly in the sweet, old-fashioned and faultlessly kept garden, and partly in the cool, softly lighted drawing-room.

Miss Marjory's guest and deputy landlord made himself most agreeable. He talked politics and science with Miss Marjory, told anecdotes and traveller's tales to Ethel, and discussed town talk with Horace, who had not long left London for Whitbury.

When Tor reached his room that night, it

was with the consciousness that he had made at least one valuable friend, but at the same time with the fear that his position was gradually growing less and less secure. Troublesome reflections would crowd into his mind, and it was anything but a pleasant possibility that loomed before him, the thought that he might be branded as a felon and taste the sweets of convict-life! That would be rather a heavy penalty to pay for the fraud he had practised for friendship's sake; and yet it was just possible that an adverse fate might drive matters even to such a crisis as that. What then would become of his intended proposal to Maud? She would be as hopelessly beyond his reach as if she were the wife of Lewis Belassis. The reflection was not inspiriting, but Tor shook himself, ' pulled himself together,' and smiled at his own depression.

'Never say die! What can have come to me? There's no reason why I should be betrayed, or betray myself. Old Belassis will have enough on his hands, I should say, after my hints, without trying to upset my claim. I wonder what Miss Marjory knows about him. I must have some more conversation with her to-morrow. She is a clever woman, I am sure ; and will, I think, stand my friend.'

So Tor argued himself out of his fears, and soon regained his customary elasticity of spirit. He slept soundly, and woke in a happier frame of mind.

He and Miss Marjory made the breakfast-table very lively ; and when she requested him to make a tour of inspection round house and gardens, Ethel and Horace smiled at one another, and said that Cousin Marjory had evidently made a conquest, and would have no trouble in getting her own way with the landlord, even were her demands more ex-orbitant than they were known to be.

Very brisk and business-like did Miss Marjory show herself as she conducted 'Mr. Debenham' round 'his friend's' property. No smallest allusion did she make to what had passed between them on the previous afternoon, but confined herself exclusively to the matter in hand. She showed what had been done in house and garden since her father had taken out the lease, explained what she wanted done now, and discussed with him what she considered to be her share of the undertaking, and what she believed the landlord should be ready to do. Her demands were both just and reasonable, and Tor assented readily to all she proposed, and would have even done more, only that Miss Marjory checked him.

'Oh no, thank you. I don't wish to be extortionate; and besides, that would be wasteful. I don't say but what the stables might have been better arranged originally; but they have done very well for us these twenty-eight years, and will do so till the end of the chapter. There's no end to the expense when once you begin to dabble in bricks and mortar; and if you take my advice you'll let the matter alone. I've told you what I want—the well, and the iron fencing, and general outside repairs. You will have to spend a good deal over those. Don't run into needless expense.'

'Well, Miss Marjory, I will be guided by your judgment; but you have done so much yourself, that it would be shabby of me not to be willing to meet you more than

half-way. Look at all the glass you have
put up.'

' Yes; that's my hobby. I can't do without flowers; and when you once begin, you
must go on. There's no end to what one
wants. I should like to have seven acres of
glass, like Veitch.'

' And overlook all yourself, Miss Marjory ?'
asked Tor, with a smile.

' Yes, of course. I always do want my
finger in everybody's pie. I suppose you
think I couldn't do it—an old woman like
me.'

' I have a very strong impression that you
could do anything you've a mind to, Miss
Marjory,' answered Tor; and Miss Marjory
laughed and shook her head at him in implied
rebuke.

' Trying to practise on the credulity of an
old woman, Mr. Debenham. As if I did not
know all your tricks by heart--idle young
good-for-nothings! Come now, we have not
quite done our business yet. I have told my
factotum tradesman to meet you here to-day,
to give you a sort of general estimate as to
time and cost. You will find him a very

honest and capable man, this Alfred Belassis, and you cannot do better than employ him.'

Tor's eyes opened wide.

'What name did you say?'

'Alfred Belassis; he is quite our model tradesman in Whitbury, for anything in the building line, within or without—a capital workman, though still young.'

Tor was looking hard at Miss Marjory.

'Alfred Belassis!' he said slowly. 'Alfred Belassis! How very curious!'

'Yes, it is rather curious, isn't it?' said Miss Marjory coolly ; 'the same name as that uncle of your friend's—of yours, I mean—of whom you think so highly. He will be here shortly, and my advice to you is—*look well at him.*'

The significance of the last four words convinced Tor that Miss Marjory knew, or suspected, more than a mere coincidence in this identity of names ; but no more was said then, for the said Alfred Belassis was already approaching them, having been directed by the servants to the spot where Miss Marjory and the landlord were consulting together.

The talk that followed was chiefly carried

on between the tradesman and Miss Marjory, Tor contenting himself by assenting to what was proposed, and throwing in an observation from time to time for form's sake. He followed Miss Marjory's advice to the letter, however, and looked well at Belassis, bestowing such careful scrutiny upon him as would have astonished him, had he been made aware of it.

Yes, Tor was quite convinced that there was some vague likeness between this young builder and Philip's Uncle Belassis. There was something similar in build and in voice; and several little tricks of manner were strongly alike. The younger man was a far pleasanter specimen of humanity, quiet, civil, and unassuming, yet thoroughly up to his work, and able to grasp Miss Marjory's meaning, and even to make notes, in spite of her rapid delivery, which puzzled Tor more than once.

So he watched attentively, and the conviction became stronger, and a sense of vague bewilderment grew up, as he traced more and more of the Belassis form and colouring in this Whitbury tradesman who bore their name.

What it could all mean, he was at a loss to imagine.

When Belassis was gone, Miss Marjory turned round with something of triumph in her tone.

'Well, and what do you say to that? What have you made out there?'

'He must come of the same stock, I think,' said Tor slowly. 'He certainly is rather like my uncle, unless my fancy has deceived me.'

'I do not imagine that it has,' said Miss Marjory significantly.

'You believe he belongs to that family?' asked Tor. 'I have never heard of him!'

'Probably not.'

'You think, as a poor relation, he has been kept in the background purposely?'

'Alfred Belassis is by no means a poor man. He is very well-to-do in the world.'

'But still in trade.'

'Yes, in trade ; but do you think a wealthy man, even in trade, would be quite beneath Alfred Belassis' notice?'

'I see you know more than I do, Miss Marjory,' said Tor, the feeling of perplexity growing slowly upon him. 'Won't you confide in me now, and tell me what it is?'

'Come into the shrubbery, then, where we can talk uninterrupted. I do not know much, but I suspect a good deal. Perhaps we can piece it together.'

Tor followed her, wondering, but not seeing the end. Was this what she meant by 'putting a spoke in Belassis' wheel'?

'Now,' said Miss Marjory, seating herself upon a rustic chair, and bidding Tor follow her example. 'I suppose, as you are a man, you don't see an inch before your nose as yet? Men never do.'

Tor was forced to admit that he didn't.

'Now, who do you suppose was the father of that young man?'

'Was it a brother of Belassis?—a brother who made a low marriage and was cast off, and never heard of more? That's what I fancy must have taken place.'

'Well, you might have made a worse shot,' returned Miss Marjory indulgently. 'However, you haven't quite got to the rights of it yet, as you will see when I tell you that the

father's name was the same as the son's—
Alfred Belassis.'

' Alfred Belassis !'

' Yes, Alfred Belassis, brothers are not
usually called by the same name.'

' A cousin ?' suggested Tor feebly ; but
Miss Marjory cut him ruthlessly short.

' Cousin, indeed ! Don't make yourself out
denser than you are ! I believe you have
grasped the situation now.'

' Do you mean that you think he is my
uncle's son ?' quoth Tor. ' Impossible !'

' I believe he is Philip Debenham's uncle's
son, most assuredly ; and so will you too, if you
will only listen to me.'

' But has he, then, a right to his name ?'
Tor could not help asking. ' Do you mean
that Belassis has been twice married ?'

' Oh yes, he was married fast enough. Mr.
Longmore married them—my pretty waiting-
maid, Nelly Roberts, and that young loafer
Alfred Belassis, whom we none of us knew,
and none of us liked. But they would go
their own way, and nobody could hinder the
marriage. Nelly was one-and-twenty, and he
a little older. He made out that he was well-

to-do, and would make a lady of her ; and her silly head was turned, and they got married, and lived for a few months at the Angler's Arms, where he had been stopping for the fishing. And then one fine morning he got some letters from home, he told her, and must go away for a few days on business. He left no address, saying he would write when he reached his destination, and she was too confiding to ask questions. He went away in gay good spirits, and never returned again ; nor did any word or message from him ever reach her from that day forward.'

' The scoundrel !' muttered Tor.

' So we all said,' assented Miss Marjory—' all but Nelly, who was convinced that some evil chance had befallen him. There had been a bad coaching accident somewhere in the country on the day he had left her, and she was fully per- suaded that he had been killed in it. Nobody else believed this theory, for we had none of us liked the young man, who was vulgar and pretentious, without having anything to re- commend him. I told Nelly that no doubt his movements could be traced, and her sus- picion either verified or overthrown ; and that

if he was still living he could be made to
support her.   But her pride revolted against
such a course.   She showed what I considered
a very proper spirit, and said that if he had
left her of his own free will, he might leave
her.   She would never force herself where she
was not wanted, and make him support her,
now that he was tired of her, and despised her
love.   If he was dead, as she believed,
search would be useless ; and if not, she would
still not have him found.   He could come
back to her of his own accord if he would ; if
not, he might stay away, and she would never
trouble him more.   We Whitbury people
believed she had judged wisely for herself—
such a marriage could only end in unhappiness
—and we all pitied and helped her, for she
was an orphan, poor child, and had no relatives in the neighbourhood.'

Tor was listening intently, an uncomfortable
feeling growing up in his mind.

' Did she live long ?' he asked.   ' I suppose
she is not alive now ?'

' No.   She lived several years though, and
brought up her little boy, Alfred, well and
respectably ; but when he was about four or

five years old, as nearly as I can remember, her health failed very much, and the charge of the child became more of a burden than she could undertake. I found a home for the boy in an institution, where he would be well cared for, and taught a useful trade; and his mother, quite satisfied, went to live with some relatives in the South of England, who had offered her a home. I heard from her from time to time, and then I went abroad for a couple of years, during which period her letters quite ceased. When I came back, and could make inquiries, I found out that she had died, though how and when, I do not exactly know.'

When she had died was, in Tor's mind, an important point. Miss Marjory and he were both thinking the same thing.

' Do you know when your uncle's second marriage took place?' asked Miss Marjory abruptly.

' I have been considering—I think it must have been in or very much about the year 1850.'

' Nelly Belassis was living in November, 1849,' remarked Miss Marjory—' living, and

in fair health, for I heard from her then. I
do not know how long she lived afterwards.'

'But surely Belassis knew,' said Tor. 'He
is a villain, and a clumsy villain, too ; but I
think he knows better than to perpetrate
bigamy. He must have kept his eye upon
her, and verified her death.'

'It is possible, of course ; but I do not
know how he managed it, if he did. Nelly
never heard one syllable from him during the
years that followed the desertion, and you may
be sure he would not let his face be seen in
Whitbury. He had left too many bad debts
behind him, perpetrated too many questionable
actions, in addition to his conduct towards
poor Nelly, ever to care to appear here
again in a hurry. When Nelly left, I believe
nobody but myself knew whither she had
gone; so that, even if he did start an inquiry
after her, there is every probability he would
have been baffled. It is my very firm impression that he just looked upon his doings here
as a crop of wild oats that he had sown in his
youth ; and trusted to the thousand and one
chances of life, that if ever there came to be a

harvest, it would not be his hand that would reap it.'

Tor thought this supposition quite in keeping with the clumsy rascality of Belassis, as he had seen it. He had no opinion at all of Phil's uncle's capacity. His wife's shrewdness and his own dogged determination and brazen dishonesty had carried him safely on so far, when not opposed by any far-seeing or strongminded foe ; but he could quite believe him capable of running a tremendous risk rather than lose a present opportunity of good, or face a distinctly awkward position.

' You may be right,' he said slowly. ' He is a pitiful coward, and as covetous as Judas. I suppose to have acknowledged such a marriage would have ruined his prospects for life.'

' Just so. I imagine his father would have had scant mercy, if it had come to his ears.'

' If Belassis takes after his father, I should say he would.'

There was a pause for reflection.

' I suppose you do not know much of this uncle's past history ?'

' No, little enough. The real Phil might

know more, perhaps, though I don't think it would come to much. I could find out, though, I dare say.'

' From whom ?'

' From Mrs. Lorraine, my aunt *pro tem.* Mrs. Belassis' sister, and Mrs. Debenham's.'

' From what you tell me of your mother's family—I mean, of course, Mr. Debenham's mother's family—they seem very well born people—quite superior to the Belassis'.'

' Yes, quite, I should say.'

' Then what made one of the sisters marry Alfred Belassis ?'

' That I don't know, but I might find out.'

' Do so if you can. Of course, a match like that would be an immense advantage to a man in his position ; one can understand that if such a thing as that were in view, he would be reluctant enough to confess his former marriage with a lady's-maid. I wonder if Nelly was dead at the time, and if he knew it. Mr. Debenham, unless you can make sure of that fact, don't let your sister marry Lewis Belassis on any account.'

' I will not,' said Tor resolutely.

' You must find out the exact date of the

wedding, and I will endeavour to find out that of Nelly's death. Unluckily, as all these things happened more than a quarter of a century ago, I am doubtful if I have even a record left of the place the poor girl went to. It was Devonshire or Dorsetshire, I think, but I can be sure of nothing. Still, I will do my best ; where there's a will there's a way. And I think you have now another hold upon your worthy uncle.'

'I think so,' answered Tor, with some satisfaction in his tone. 'If I wish to be specially agreeable to him, or if he has been particularly pleasant to me, I can tell him that I have been over to Whitbury, and ask him if he has any knowledge of the place.'

Miss Marjory seemed to enjoy the idea of this question very much.

'Yes, Whitbury must recall many very pleasant associations ; for, as I tell you, he sowed plenty of wild oats here before he spoilt poor Nelly's life. Mr. Graves could, I fancy, lay his hands upon some papers which would be rather disconcerting to a man of his social standing. You could ask him if he remembers the lawyer Mr. Graves, or Miss Marjory

Descartes.　I should like to see his face if you did!'

'Did he know you, then?'

'Oh, he knew me well enough to come and beg my intercession with Mr. Graves, for his poor dear Nelly's sake.　I was a silly young thing in those days, with more money than wisdom; and I was fond of Nelly, and did not want her to know what a precious sort of fellow this husband of hers was.　So I gave him money, and got him off somehow; but I don't imagine his gratitude would teach him to welcome me very warmly now.'

Tor smiled to himself.

'I could go on to sing your praises, and to assert my hope that some day I might see you at Ladywell.　May I really hope that you will visit us there one of these days?'

'I'll come if you want me—if things are going badly with you, and a curb is wanted for Belassis.　I'll come if my support will be of service to you; but I don't often pay visits for pleasure.　I always find that I wish myself home again in two days' time.'

'I trust you may not do that if you come to Ladywell,' said Tor gallantly.　'Such a promise almost makes a complication and danger desirable.'

'Stuff and nonsense! don't talk rubbish to an old woman like me. I'll come if I'm needed; and if not, I'll stay at home. But don't you be rash and drive Belassis to bay, or he might turn upon you. I'd advise you to say nothing about the kinsman you've found here.'

'I shall not at present, at any rate. I have no wish to drive things to a crisis; but I think I shall be able to guess by his manner whether or not he knew of his first wife's death, before his second marriage. I hope it is all right. I don't want, for the sake of wife and children, to drag up anything that would fall so hardly upon them; but I don't care how much of a dog's life I lead Belassis.'

'He deserves it all,' cried Miss Marjory, with energy; 'only be careful.'

'I will. I live in a glass house myself; but I shall certainly hold you over his head if he becomes objectionable.'

'Yes, you may do that. I rather like an encounter of wits myself. In the days of my youth I was a good hand at retort. I don't think my tongue has quite lost its cunning even now.'

' I don't think so either,' smiled Tor. ' Yes, we must certainly contrive a meeting, face to face.'

Miss Marjory would make no definite promise, but Tor went away convinced that he had gained a valuable ally, and one who would never desert him, and who would, perhaps, be more dangerous to Belassis than he himself could be.

There was something in Miss Marjory's assured position and in the respect which she always inspired, as well as in her age and experience, which was very encouraging to the young man, who certainly needed all the advantages he could secure ; and he was now exceedingly glad that the lease of his house had fallen in, and that Miss Marjory had summoned him to Whitbury.

CHAPTER II.

MRS. BELASSIS VISITS LADYWELL.

IT was on a Tuesday morning that Maud said good-bye to her brother, and saw him set out for Yorkshire; and on the Wednesday morning, whilst riding out through the great avenue, she was surprised to see her Aunt Celia, walking in her resolute way up to the house.

Mrs. Belassis seldom visited Ladywell, and never before had she been there at so unseasonable an hour. Maud looked wonderingly at her, and stopped her horse, as she met the business-like figure.

'Do you want anybody, Aunt Celia?' she asked. "You will only find Aunt Olive at home. Phil has gone into Yorkshire, but he will be back this evening. Can I do anything for you?'

'Your brother is away, is he?' asked Mrs. Belassis, as though surprised. In reality she was perfectly well aware of the fact. Had her nephew been at home, she would not have taken the trouble to pay this visit.

'Yes; but he comes back to-night. Can I give him any message?'

Mrs. Belassis seemed to consider.

'Well, as I am so near I will go on and see your Aunt Olive,' she said indifferently. 'I had a question I wished to ask Philip; but that can wait. I will not interrupt you, my dear. I hope you will have a pleasant ride.'

Maud rode on, a disdainful look crossing her pretty face.

'I wonder if Aunt Celia is up to anything,' she mused. 'She generally is when she smiles and says "my dear," and puts on her gracious air. How I do loathe Aunt Celia! I do believe she is worse than Uncle Belassis. I am afraid she is Phil's enemy—not that that matters much, for she couldn't do him any harm. Sometimes I fancy Phil has something on his mind; but I don't see that he need. I wonder why he said yesterday that he was sure Aunt Olive and I would always stand his friends, through thick and thin. I should think I just would!' and Maud's eyes flashed. 'I'd stand by him whatever happened—whatever he'd said or done, or whatever people said of him. There's nobody like my Phil. I love his little finger better than all the rest of the world put together. If ever he is in any danger, won't I show him how I love him!'

Maud's whole face glowed, and she urged her horse to a gallop in her generous enthusiasm, and rode far and fast that day.

Mrs. Belassis walked boldly up to the house. She did not ring the bell, although she was on anything but intimate terms with the household at Ladywell ; she preferred to walk straight into the great hall, where she paused and looked about her.

Nobody was in sight. Neither manservant nor maidservant, bond nor free, had observed her entrance, and with a certain snake-like look of satisfaction, she quietly crossed the hall, and entered a small room which looked over the garden, and which generally went by the name of ' Phil's den.'

Once inside this room, she closed the door softly and stealthily, and looked for a moment as though she would have locked it too ; but on second thoughts she seemed to decide against doing so, and muttering, ' It might look suspicious if anyone should come,' turned away.

The room was not large, and was furnished quite in bachelor fashion, with a shabby but luxuriously easy leather chair, a multitude of pipes and cigar - boxes ; one small table beside the easy-chair, which was strewn with newspapers and smoking apparatus, and a large writing-table full of drawers which stood in the window. The walls were adorned by guns and fishing-tackle, and by some engravings which showed greater taste for art, and less for sport, than do most bachelors' pictures. It was a snug, cosy room ; and the presence of a second and much daintier arm-chair, in the opposite corner, seemed to indicate that Maud liked at times to be her brother's ' den companion.'

Mrs. Belassis' keen eye took all this in at a glance. She saw in a moment where lay her work, and she seated herself in a quiet business-like way at the writing-table.

'It will be rather odd,' she muttered to herself, 'if amongst all his papers I do not find something to give me a clue, if there is anything wrong, and I'm not generally deceived when I take an idea into my head.'

Mrs. Belassis set to work in a methodical way. She began with the small drawers at the top of the table, and turned the contents rapidly over, spreading out the papers and glancing quickly over them. She did not seem to find anything of any interest amongst these, and in ten minutes that part of her search was completed.

It was with greater deliberation that she commenced to open the larger drawers on either side of her; and her face was more set, her eyes more curious than ever, as this task proceeded.

First came papers and memoranda connected with the Ladywell property, bills, receipts, correspondence as to cattle, hay, poultry, and the thousand and one transactions necessitated by a farm and estate. Tor was not a specially

orderly man, but he had a method of classi-
fication with his papers, which enabled him
to lay his hand readily upon anything he
wanted.

A few minutes' study convinced Mrs.
Belassis that there was nothing to be gained
by a minute inspection of these papers, so
they were replaced in their drawer, and the
next one opened.

This contained private bills and correspondence, and Mrs. Belassis looked as if she
anticipated considerable information from the
heap of papers she drew out.

' Extravagant !' she muttered more than
once ; a dark look crossing her face as she
came across receipted bills for dresses, jewellery,
and finery of all kinds for Maud, and handsome silks and laces, in which she knew her
sister Olive had appeared.

Still, amongst all these bills and papers
she did not seem to find what she wanted,
although more than enough to annoy and
anger her. The letters were all addressed to
' Philip Debenham, Esq.,' and were for the
most part petitions from charitable institu-
tions, notices from picture-dealers, or offers

of everything for nothing from companies and
tradespeople.

These papers were replaced in their drawer,
and the search continued.

The third drawer upon that side was
locked, so with rather a significant smile
Mrs. Belassis tried the first on the next side.
This opened readily enough, but merely contained a supply of writing-paper, envelopes,
stamps, and pens, which, by its orderly
appearance, seemed to have been given over to
Maud's willing care. The drawer below contained the farm-books, the garden-book and
the stable-book, which had been kept with
scrupulous exactness by old Mr. Maynard,
and which his successor had taken some
apparent pains to keep in their old accuracy
under a new *régime.*

The third drawer, again, was locked.

' These must be the two that I want,' said
Mrs. Belassis under her breath ; and again she
glanced towards the door, as though she would
have liked to lock it, but considered it more
prudent to abstain.

A looker-on might have been tempted to
wonder how Mrs. Belassis proposed to get at

the contents of those locked drawers. Was she going to force the locks? Not at all. Whatever her husband might be, Mrs. Belassis was never clumsy. What she undertook to do, was done neatly, and even artistically.

Ladies of some social standing do not usually visit their friends' houses with skeleton-keys hidden away in their pockets; but it was nothing more nor less than this useful little implement that Mrs. Belassis drew out now; and with the snake-like look more visible than ever in her eyes, she set about her task.

Kneeling down upon the floor, she soon had the first drawer open, and had taken from thence the documents it held.

There was Phil's cheque-book first of all, and then a few papers folded and held together by an elastic band. There was a bag, which evidently held some money, and behind all these some papers and relics, which were evidently all that had come to him from the effects of the father and mother. Belassis had taken care that such mementoes should be but few.

The cheque-book first claimed Mrs. Belassis'

earnest attention. She studied the counterfoils closely, and then began comparing the
sums with the amounts upon the bills she
had previously found. Naturally they corre-
sponded accurately enough; but what Mrs.
Belassis noticed was this, that for at least
six bills (all presents for Maud) which were
specified to have been settled ' by cheque,' no
counterfoil was to be found : and this fact
seemed significant of something, though of
what she could not yet say.

Next the family relics were contemptuously
turned over, and put back in their place,
and Mrs. Belassis now commenced the
study of the papers enclosed by the elastic
band.

There were but two of them after all,
though one was of a bulk and importance
that gave it the substance of half a dozen
ordinary letters. The crabbed characters were
familiar to her eye, and it did not need the
colossal signature ' T. M. Maynard ' to tell
her that it had been penned by her late uncle,
the former master of Ladywell.

It was, in fact, nothing less than the dead
man's letter to his nephew, Philip Debenham,

which Tor had read in the little hotel at Hornberg.

With a subdued exclamation of curiosity and satisfaction, Mrs. Belassis sat down to read the document ; and as she did so, her face assumed an expression not at all agreeable to look upon. She read the paper not once, but twice ; and the venomous expression deepened upon her face, until it grew positively hideous in its intensity.

Then she turned the paper over and over, and opened out its stiff folds, although the writing had only occupied the first page, and in so doing her attention was caught by a few pencilled words written on the inside, as if by an afterthought. And she was convinced by the manner in which the paper opened, that hers had been the first hand which had unfolded it. An eager yet dark look crossed her face, as she took in the sense of that aftermessage.

' Your father once gave me to understand that he had drawn up a more equitable will, and had hidden it away somewhere in my library. I told him he had better take it out and give it to a lawyer to keep. And I think

he must have taken it out—and destroyed it;
for I never could find it, though I took the
trouble to make a thorough search. He was
just a muddler with his affairs, and a dreamer
too. You may be sure he made away with
the will in a moment of weakness; but of
course if you choose to search for it, you
can—you won't find it.'

As she took in the import of these words,
Mrs. Belassis fairly trembled. The anger
which had disfigured her face before, gave way
now to a look more nearly approaching terror;
and then, after a few minutes of deep thought,
she folded the paper once more and put it in
her pocket.

' I will show it to Alfred. He must see it.
Then the pencilled words shall be erased, and
I will take an early opportunity to return the
paper. There are a hundred chances to one
that it will not be missed. Now for the other.'

The other was Maud's eager letter to her
brother, written to him at Hornberg, to
announce her delight and eager anticipation.
The terms in which it was couched were not
calculated to soothe Mrs. Belassis, and a look
of bitter hatred crossed her face.

'The little reptile, the little toad—making mischief from the very first! Oh, but I will be even with her! She shall learn to rue the day when first she tried to poison her brother's minds against us—putting all sorts of suspicions into his head. Faugh! the ingratitude of the little viper!'

Mrs. Belassis folded the letter, and flung it into the drawer after the other things, and then she viciously locked it. Her mind was so much disturbed by her late discoveries, that she was almost tempted to pursue her researches no further, confident that she had found the most important papers in existence. But the dogged stubbornness of her character prevailed over her preoccupation and dismay, and she remembered that although she had found something of the greatest importance, she had not found anything of the character she had hoped—nothing to compromise her nephew, or to verify the very dim suspicion that had entered into her head. What that suspicion was she would have found it hard to say ; all that she told even herself as yet was that there was 'something odd' about Phil, and that she believed there was ' some mystery ' going on.

So far, however, she had found nothing to encourage such an idea, and with a certain sense of having been baffled, she opened the sixth and last drawer.

There were not many papers here ; but there was a second cheque-book, and upon the inside of the cover was written ' Tor's cheque-book.' There was also a bank-book labelled ' Torrington Torwood, Esq. ;' and rapid reference to the former showed Mrs. Belassis that the missing counterfoils of cheques she knew to have been written by Phil, were to be found, not in his, but in Mr. Torwood's cheque-book.

This was something of a facer, and she felt a triumphant joy in finding anything so like a mystery. She did not pause now to try and unravel it, but passed on to the other contents of the drawer.

There were two letters from a certain ' Marjory Descartes,' asking Phil to go over to ' Whitbury ' to settle some business for Mr. Torwood, and there were one or two business communications from agents or bankers, referring to Phil some question about Mr. Torwood's affairs. These were read with a certain sense of disappointment, as they seemed

to show that Phil was openly acting as his
friend's agent ; but hope rose again when a
deeper dive into the drawer brought out a little
packet of papers, some quite old and yellow,
which proved to be I O U's for various sums,
all signed ' Philip Debenham.'

' Moneys Mr. Torwood lent him, evidently,'
mused Mrs. Belassis. ' Oh, then Phil's friend
was not quite so disinterested, after all, as we
were led to think. I thought there was something odd about it. But how comes Phil to
have these papers now? There is no evidence
that he has redeemed them. It is a large sum
—nearly £3,000, I should say. His cheque-
book shows no mention of Mr. Torwood, and
I should have heard from Alfred, I think, if
he had handed over any very large sum
whilst the securities were being settled. I
don't understand why he keeps them if they
are redeemed, and why he has not a receipt
for the amount if it is paid. If not, how
comes he by the papers at all?'

Certainly, what with one thing and what
with another, Mrs. Belassis had ample food
for meditation ; but she had stayed so long
that she feared to linger. She locked up the

drawer, and was preparing to leave, when Maud came suddenly in, in her riding-habit.

'Aunt Celia, you here!' she exclaimed. 'Have you been here all this while? Aunt Olive says she has never even seen you. What can you have been doing all this time? Two whole hours !'

Maud looked both excited and suspicious. This was her house, and she was mistress ; and she considered that her Aunt Celia had taken a great liberty in making her way in unobserved, and shutting herself up in Phil's den. Her face showed as much very plainly.

Mrs. Belassis looked at her with her cold smile.

' Do not act and speak like a spoilt child, my dear. It is not becoming to a young mistress. I fear you are forgetting the lessons I instilled into your mind at Thornton House.'

' Oh, there is no fear of my forgetting your lessons or Thornton House either,' cried Maud, with what sounded very like defiance in her tone. ' But I hope I have shaken off the effects of that yoke. What I want to know is, why you have been shut up in Phil's room for two hours—in his *private* room.'

23—2

Mrs. Belassis looked at the indignant Maud with a smile of cool disdain.

'As this is your brother's house, over which you preside, I will condescend to reply, otherwise I should decline to answer such an insolent interrogation. After I left you I made a tour of the gardens and hot-houses, which I am never invited to inspect, of course, owing to the kind politeness of the mistress of Ladywell. After I had enjoyed the sweetness of the flowers and trees for above an hour, I came here to write a note to Philip; but what I wrote did not satisfy me, and I tore up the letter and determined to wait till I could see him personally. Just as I was about to leave the room my niece entered, and here we are now, face to face. Are you satisfied?'

'I don't know,' answered Maud; 'but I hear what you say. Are you going? Good-bye. If you care to see Aunt Olive she is in the drawing-room. We shall have lunch in an hour.'

'I will go home, thank you,' said Mrs. Belassis coldly. 'Good-bye, my dear.'

Maud watched her cross the hall, a distrustful and angry light in her eyes.

'She always gets the best of it with me. I can never be politely cutting to Aunt Celia, as Phil is. I am always rude, and she makes me feel like a schoolgirl. How I detest her! I wonder why she came. I know what she said was all lies. What can she have been up to? I wonder what that letter to Phil was that she wrote and destroyed. Did she write a letter at all?' Maud went forward and carefully looked about for torn fragments of paper, but could find none.

'If she wrote it she took it away in her pocket,' said Maud; and then she opened the ink-bottle and saw that it had been washed out that morning and not refilled. Mrs. Belassis had certainly written no letter there that day. What she had done, the girl was at a loss to imagine. All that she could tell was that her aunt's visit was certain to mean mischief of some kind.

Mrs. Belassis had ample food for reflection on her homeward way, and very earnestly did she strive to form some theory as to the respective position of Phil and his friend, so as to prove, if possible, that the former was acting in a reprehensible manner.

At last an idea was hit upon which seemed
to satisfy her; at any rate, it gave a semblance
of reality to her suspicions.

'I believe he has got his friend shut up in
a lunatic asylum somewhere—unless he has
put him out of the way altogether; and he
is playing a double game—sometimes Torwood and sometimes himself. I suppose he
was Torwood abroad, whilst he was the rich
man; and here he is Debenham; thus reaping
the benefits of both characters. Perhaps Mr.
Torwood's mind has been failing of late, so
that he has learned to depend upon Philip;
yes, that is very likely. And now that he
has money of his own, he has just disposed
of his friend anyhow—no doubt in a mad-
house—and is figuring about here as a great
man, and spending his friend's money as well
as his own. Oh, you're a nice young man,
Philip Debenham! No wonder you keep
your friend at a distance, and don't trouble
yourself about him. No wonder nobody can
get to know anything definite about the
"Tor" who was once all your talk. A very
nice thing it will be for you when I bring
it home to you! Oh yes, you will enjoy that

very much; and I wonder what the law will say to these little transactions with Torwood's money ;' and in this strain Mrs. Belassis kept on, her spirits rising and her confidence in her theory increasing with every step she took. But when she felt in her pocket, and her hand came in contact with the stiff paper it held, her face changed suddenly, and the old look of rage and fear returned.

'If old Maynard is right, if there is another will, and if that will is ever found—then we shall be ruined! Why did I ever marry such a fool as Alfred Belassis? I could do anything if it were not for his clumsiness!'

CHAPTER III.

THE MISSING PAPER.

TOR did not return to Ladywell until late at night, having missed a train at one of the junctions, where his cross route obliged him to change.

Maud, therefore, said nothing to him about Mrs. Belassis' strange behaviour until the following afternoon, when they rode out together, and then she told him as much as she knew of this oddly-timed visit.

'Wanted to see me, did she?' said Tor. 'I wonder what for. I'll call at Thornton House this evening and ask. I can walk over after dinner.'

'Oh no, don't!' cried Maud coaxingly. 'The evenings are so dull without you. Never mind Aunt Celia. She is quite horrid.

Let her come again if she wants you. I believe it was just a lie.'

'Come, little sister, don't be spiteful. I know Mrs. Belassis does not greatly love either of us, still we must be civil as long as we can, or we put ourselves at a disadvantage.'

'I know I do,' assented Maud. 'I can't manage as you do; I wish I could. She would give anything to be able to put you into a rage as she puts me; but she never can.'

Tor smiled calmly.

'Just so; and I have no intention of affording her that gratification.'

'It must be nice to be a man—a man like you, I mean,' said Maud, regarding him with a loving admiration distinctly flattering to its object. Then, after a pause, she added, 'I wonder what Aunt Celia really came for.'

'You think she had some ulterior motive?'

'I don't need to think—I *know* she had,' cried Maud. 'I saw it by the look in her eye — just like a snake. I haven't lived eighteen years in Thornton House for nothing, Phil.'

'Phil' rode on in silence, wondering if there could be any truth in Maud's surmise; for he was convinced that Mrs. Belassis was his enemy, and a more dangerous one than her husband.

Pondering, however, did not bring him any nearer the truth; so he gave up puzzling his head about the matter, and determined to take this opportunity to speak to Maud about Lewis Belassis.

'Maud,' he began, 'when is your birthday?'

'Three weeks next Wednesday,' answered the girl promptly.

'And you will then be twenty-four?'

'Yes.'

Maud looked at him, and he looked at her, and then she broke into a little soft laugh.

'You dear old Phil, you are so handsome! I wish I could marry you!'

A curious thrill ran through Tor, and his eyes were eloquent, but he only answered coolly enough :

'But as you cannot—what then, Maud?'

'I don't know,' she answered; and her face took the spoilt-child expression which thoughts of Lewis Belassis almost always brought.

'You have not made up your mind?'

'No; I can't.

'But it will be expected of you soon, will it not?'

'Yes, I suppose so. I know on my birthday I am to hear the will read, and a letter papa left with it for me. I believe I shall be expected to give my answer then, though the money can't be divided till a little while later. Phil, do you think it would be unfair to Lewis to keep him waiting any longer?'

'I don't think you'll gain anything by waiting, Maud. I should say the wisest plan would be to get the matter off your mind, one way or the other, as soon as you can. I imagine you'll feel exactly as you do now, a year hence, in regard to Lewis. If you haven't fallen in love with him all these years, you are hardly likely to do so now.'

'I should never be *in love* with Lewis— never!' cried Maud, almost disdainfully. 'Fancy feeling sentimental over a man like that! But then, I do like him, and I might never meet anyone I liked so well ; and there is my money, you know.'

'Don't think about the money, Maud,' said Tor quickly.   He would have liked to promise there and then, that she should never feel the need of that—to tell her that he would make the loss good ; but he could hardly hand over £10,000 of Phil's money so coolly, even though he felt sure of his ultimate approval : and gladly as he would have sacrificed his own fortune to her, he knew that there was only one way by which his wealth could be made hers, and that way was, as yet, closed to him.

'I can't help thinking about it,' answered Maud. 'If I had come of age at twenty-one, as other girls do, I should not have thought as I do now.   Five thousand would have seemed riches, and love in a cottage the ideal of bliss. I should have sent Lewis about his business in double-quick time then, and bought the little cottage behind Roma's studio, and lived there in glorious independence.   At twenty-one we know nothing of life, and are filled to the brim with romance.   But three more years teach us a good deal ;' and Maud shook her head gravely.   'Things take very different proportions, and we see that life isn't just what we pictured. Do you think papa knew that when he fixed my majority ?'

' No ; but I have no doubt Belassis did.'

' Uncle Belassis !' cried Maud. ' What has he to do with it ?'

' Everything, I imagine. Do you suppose our father would have made such an iniquitous will except under compulsion ?'

Maud's face changed visibly.

' But Uncle Belassis says——'

' *That* for what he says.'

Gradually Maud seemed to take in the true meaning of Tor's words.

' Oh !' she said, and stopped short. ' Oh ! so that's how it was ! I wonder I did not think of it before. Phil, you don't want me to marry Lewis Belassis?'

' Perhaps not ; but I wish you to decide for yourself—to be guided by your own wishes.'

Tor was anxious, if possible, not to interfere in Maud's decision. He had a strong hope that she would of her own accord reject Lewis.

' Papa wished it,' she said, hesitating.

' Indeed !'

' You think not ? *Could* Uncle Belassis have had so much power as all that ?'

' Could your father have cared so much for a little snuffling brat of five years old, as Lewis was at the time of the making of that will ?'

Maud considered this aspect of the case with some gravity.

' Yes, he certainly would be a " little snuffling brat " at that age—I can just see him, though I can't remember him, as you can. I'll tell him some day of your description ; it is so vivid.'

' Do ; and if you want to know whether the match was approved by other members of the family, you can ask Aunt Olive what she thinks.'

' I know she doesn't like it.'

' And I have a letter at home from our great-uncle, Mr. Maynard, expressing distinct disapproval, and speaking in no measured terms of his opinion of Belassis' share in the matter.'

Maud began to look amused and interested.

' Old Uncle Maynard wrote about it, did he? Oh, you must let me see the letter ! I am sure

it will be delightfully funny ; he was such a
dear, cross old man, and I was always so cheeky
to him. The Belassis' were furious because he
took more notice of me than of anybody else,
though that didn't come to much; but I should
like to see the letter.'

' I'll show it you when we go in,' said Tor,
and then let the talk glide into other channels.
He considered that he had given Maud food for
meditation sufficient for one day, and decided
not to press for an answer, until she had well
thought over the information he had bestowed.

Maud did not forget her curiosity about her
great-uncle's letter, and as soon as they returned from their ride she followed Tor into
his study, and begged him to produce it.

' I know it will be so queer!' she said, a
smile of anticipation curving her pretty
mouth.

Tor unlocked the drawer, and put in his
hand. He took out Maud's letter with the
elastic band round it ; but no other paper
was with it. He pulled open the drawer to
its utmost limit, and looked again, but the
paper was evidently not there.

' It's gone !' he ejaculated, in some surprise.

' Try the next,' suggested Maud.

' No good,' he answered, shaking his head. ' 'Twas only the day I left, that I locked up the letters about Tor's business in the opposite drawer, where I keep everything relating to him ; and I opened this one too, and saw old Maynard's letter lying with yours, strapped together. I could take my oath of it.'

' Witchcraft!' said Maud ; and then her face grew grave suddenly, and she added significantly : ' Witchcraft, or Aunt Celia.'

' Couldn't have been Aunt Celia. The drawer was locked,' said Tor.

' Then it must have been a ghost,' said Maud seriously. ' For nobody else could have opened a locked drawer.'

The two looked at each other in silence.

' You think her capable of such an act?'

' She is capable of anything.'

Tor considered, and failed to see any motive for the robbery.

' It was a misanthropical letter, anything but complimentary to the Belassis family; but I can't see why she should have purloined it. It is not a paper they would care to study long or frequently, I imagine.'

Maud's face had clouded over.

'Aunt Celia always knows what she is about. You may be sure that that paper is of more value than you know.'

'If so,' said Tor composedly, 'I will take care to get it back pretty quickly. I am going over there to-night. In all probability I shall bring it back with me.'

Maud looked admiringly at him, but shook her head.

'You won't if Aunt Celia wants it; besides, you cannot ask for it.'

'I'm not so sure of that,' said Tor, and Maud wondered which half of the sentence he was answering.

After dinner, in the soft summer twilight, he walked over to Thornton House. Maud accompanied him through the park, but he would not let her come farther, nor be present at his interview with the aunt, about which she felt very curious.

After she had turned back, he pursued his way slowly, thinking over what he should say to her, and also to Belassis, if he should, as was not improbable, have to encounter them both. On the whole, he felt he would rather face the two together than meet them singly.

In this fortune favoured him. Lewis had taken his sisters to a dinner-party in the neighbourhood, and Mr. and Mrs. Belassis were in earnest talk together in the drawing-room, when the door was suddenly opened, and the servant announced in loud tones :

' Mr. Debenham !'

From the distinct start and shuffle that followed, Tor was convinced that he had interrupted a conversation in which his name occupied a prominent place. In nowise dis-concerted, however, he walked up and shook hands in his easiest fashion, and then sat down in such a position as commanded a good view of both the countenances before him.

' I hear you walked over to see me yesterday morning,' began Tor, addressing Mrs. Belassis. ' I am sorry you had your trouble for nothing. I have come over to learn the object of your visit, and save you the trouble of a second walk.'

' Oh, thank you—I am sorry you took the trouble. I merely came to ask if you could supply us with butter for a time. I suppose it must be the hot weather, for we cannot make half enough for ourselves just now.'

'So that was the important message that could not be trusted to paper,' said Tor, with a smile. 'Yes, certainly you shall have all you need. I will speak to the man to-morrow. I am sorry such a small affair should have occasioned you so long a walk.'

'It did not, thanks; I was close to Ladywell as it happened, and I wanted to see your aunt.'

Tor knew she had made no attempt to see Mrs. Lorraine, and his slight questioning smile said as much; but he made no open comment. Mrs. Belassis sat stonily composed. If she had any inward trepidation she gave no outward sign of it.

Tor turned to the uncle.

'We are getting almost dried up here in the south, sir. We look quite parched. In Yorkshire now, everything is beautifully fresh—though not so forward as with us.'

'You have been in Yorkshire, then?' questioned Mrs. Belassis, as if she welcomed the change of subject.

'Yes, upon some business of Mr. Torwood's.

24—2

It's a fine county, I should say, by what I saw of it. Do you know it at all, sir?'

'I—oh—Yorkshire, did you say?' said Belassis, seemingly rather flustered by the sudden query. 'Why, Yorkshire is a big place, you know. Yes, to be sure, I was there once, when I was a lad; but that's a long time ago now;' and he gave rather a sickly laugh.

Tor fancied that his wife noticed his constrained manner, and glanced curiously at him.

'It was a pretty little town I had to visit, quite an ideal place for quiet picturesqueness. Whitbury was its name. I suppose you do not know anything of it?'

Mr. Belassis' face seemed to turn all colours at once.

'Whitbury—Whitbury!' he stammered, with an immense effort to make his voice sound natural. 'No, I don't remember that name. I don't think I could ever have been there.'

'I am sure you would never have forgotten the place if you had seen it,' continued Tor. 'It is so particularly pretty. There is a fine old church there, and a river running through the valley, which is quite a resort for fishermen, I believe. I have some thoughts of going there again some day to fish. The Angler's Arms is an inviting little inn. There is something very attractive to me in a simple little English town.'

'Ah, yes—very—very much so,' answered Belassis vaguely, feeling as though an iron hand was clutching at his throat, yet experiencing an insane desire to find out whether or not this detestable nephew was talking with a purpose.

The frank affable manner gave him a dim hope that all was well; but he dared not meet the eyes which perhaps would have told him more.

'You—you—went on business for your friend, did you? How comes he to have business in Whitbury? I thought he had lived always abroad.'

'He has property in Whitbury; a very charming old house inhabited by a very charming maiden lady. The house stands in a square, and faces the Minster, but looks behind on to a lovely stretch of country. Its mistress is a particularly clever and pleasant woman—a Miss Descartes—Miss Marjory Descartes as she seems to be always called.'

Belassis' face had paled to a dull grey hue. His wife's eyes were fixed upon it curiously and unquietly. Tor continued talking in the same frank, gossiping way.

'It was some business about a new lease that took me down ; but Miss Marjory and I became great friends. She was good enough to like me, and I was charmed with her. Perhaps some day I may have the pleasure of introducing her here. I have great hopes of inducing her to visit us at Ladywell some time or other.'

The dull grey hue changed to a delicate pea-green. Tor felt a sort of compassion for the miserable man before him. He had learnt all he wished to know. This man was none other than Nelly Roberts's husband, and he had *not* made sure of her death before marrying again. Had he done that, he would hardly have been so hopelessly cowed. The discovery of a former marriage, and a low one, would be an awkward affair enough for him to face now; but would hardly account for such a depth of terror as was visible in his face.

As Tor, however, had found out what he wished, he rose to depart. His quick eyes had not been occupied altogether with the faces before him. He had caught sight of a corner of thick parchment-like paper projecting from a drawer in a small table, which was rather oddly placed in front of Mr. and Mrs. Belassis. He had heard a crackle of stiff paper as he entered the room.

By a quick, quiet movement, Tor reached forward and secured the paper ; the drawer, of course, opened as he pulled, and disclosed to his view a number of soiled bread-crumbs and some pieces of india-rubber.

'Rubbing out, by Jove!' he thought to himself, and wondered what could have been accomplished by that process. Aloud he said :

'Ah, my old uncle's letter! How curious it should be here! I had just missed it from its accustomed place. What an old misanthrope he was! Not, I suppose, that he had any idea into whose hands it would fall. How could it have been spirited here ?'

'I brought it, Philip,' answered Mrs. Belassis imperturbably. 'I was just about to return it to you. I found it by chance in your room yesterday, as I was looking for some writing-paper. Curiosity prompted me to read it, and I could not refrain from bringing it back for your uncle to see. He is slow to believe the ingratitude of the world. I think that such expressions as are put down here, by a man who always received from him a respect and consideration he was far from deserving, should do much to convince him. I must apologize for the liberty I took with your property ; but you were absent, and I thought you would not object.'

'Oh, I have not the least objection in the world,' answered Tor readily and pleasantly. 'I had merely kept the contents of the paper to myself because they were not over and above flattering to those mentioned in it. What puzzles me is how you came to chance upon the letter, as it was always kept in a locked drawer.'

'It was not there yesterday,' answered Mrs. Belassis, the glittering look coming back into her eyes. 'It was in the top right-hand drawer, where your writing-paper is stored.'

'It must have been spirited there, then,' laughed Tor, 'for I left it in the left-hand bottom one, locked up, only the day before.

Well, I will say good-night now. I think we understand each other ; and I will give instructions about the butter to-morrow.'

It was in rather a peculiarly silent and constrained fashion that Mr. and Mrs. Belassis shook hands with their genial nephew and saw him depart.

Then Belassis wiped his forehead, and sat down heavily.

' We only just got that done in time,' he said, drawing a long breath, ' Suppose he had found it before we had done our work ?'

' He would not have found it at all but for you,' answered Mrs. Belassis, with cool contempt. ' It would have been upstairs, where it ought to have been, but for your folly.'

' Mine !'

' Yes ; you would bring it down ; and now this has happened !'

' What ?'

' He knows that I have been overhauling his private papers.'

' He can't know that.'

' He does know it. He is not a fool ; besides, he said as much. If you had done as I counselled, I should have replaced the paper quietly; and if he had suspected, he could have said nothing.'

'You always think you are right, and I am wrong,' growled Belassis.

'Possibly,' answered the wife; and then, fixing her eye keenly upon him, she asked: 'And pray, what is Whitbury? and who is Miss Marjory Descartes?'

Belassis' face turned livid; but he answered with a sudden blaze of anger:

'How the devil should I know? I never heard of either one or the other before to-night.'

He flung himself passionately from the room, and Mrs. Belassis sat quite still in the twilight.

'He is trying to keep a secret from me. What a fool he is!'

CHAPTER IV.

WILD OATS.

'HERE, Maud—here is old Uncle Maynard's letter, if you want to read it!'

So said Tor, as he entered the drawing-room, after his visit to Thornton House; and Maud started up with an exclamation of pleasure at seeing him again so soon. When she took in the drift of his remark, her eyes opened wide with surprise.

'The letter, Phil? Had Aunt Celia got it, then?'

'Yes; she had *borrowed* it to show to her precious husband. She found it amongst my writing-paper, she says.'

'That's a lie,' said Maud, with the frankness of her nature; 'for I tidied out that drawer the day you went to Whitbury.'

'And I left the paper locked up that same day,' added Tor, smiling. 'Aunt Celia must have a vivid imagination.'

'Did you tell her she was lying?' asked Maud eagerly. 'I mean, did you say that it was in the locked drawer?'

'There was no need to say very much. Mrs. Belassis is not dense. She quite understood me. It is better to avoid saying disagreeable things, when meaning them does as well.'

'I always want to say them,' answered Maud candidly. 'But isn't she dreadful? She must have a duplicate key of your table. Do you think she has taken anything else?'

'I shall look and see to-morrow. I don't think there is anything in that table that she would care to possess. What beats me, is the motive for taking that letter. It is disagreeable enough, but of no value. Read it, Maud, and see if you can find out anything which could explain her deed.'

Maud obeyed. After reading a little way she became so much amused that she turned again to the beginning, and read it out aloud, so that Aunt Olive might have the benefit of the joke. She enjoyed vastly the old man's misanthropic utterances, and her comments as she read amused the listeners as much as did the letter itself.

'Dear, cross old Uncle Maynard!' she exclaimed. 'Isn't it splendid how Uncle Belassis outwitted himself by keeping you away, Phil? How savage they must have been when they saw what he says! Oh, I really am glad Aunt Celia found it—it does so serve them right! He must have hated the Belassis family. I always thought he did. Do you think he's really right about the will? Did Uncle Belassis make papa put that condition in, Phil? If he did, that settles the matter. I won't have anything to do with a plot of Uncle Belassis' making. I'll send Lewis to the right-about pretty quick, if I'm just to be made a dupe of that horrid Belassis.'

Maud's cheek had flushed. Her eyes sparkled with anger.

'"Women will marry anything," will they? Well, I'll not marry Lewis to please his father —nothing shall persuade me. Yes, Phil; uncle was right. If you had not come back in time I might have been half bullied, half coaxed into it—for I do like Lewis, and I hate a row; but if you'll back me I don't care for anything, and I'll defy Uncle Belassis to his face !'

Tor smiled and stood beside the girl, who had risen in her excitement, and was standing erect and indignant, with the letter held fast in her hands. He put his hand upon her shoulder and looked down into her face.

' All right, little sister. You need have no fears on that point. You and I are more than a match for old Belassis ; and you shall neither be bullied nor coaxed into doing anything you do not like—I will take good care of that. But leave the open defiance to me ; and content yourself with the calm *hauteur* of the *grande dame.'*

Maud's face took a different expression, and the angry light died out of her eyes. She looked up at him with a grateful admiration.

' You are just an angel-boy, Phil. I wish I could be like you; but I'm afraid I shall never be the *grande dame,* I'm much too quick-tempered and volatile ; I can't think how you can keep so cool. I wish I could. I wish I were like you.'

' So do not I—I like you as you are, Maud,' answered Tor. ' But I am not going

to let you make any important decision as to
your future in a moment of heat. You must
think the matter over dispassionately, and
come calmly to your decision. But you see
what the old fellow says about my duty. You
are not to be a loser by your decision, Maud.
A wish like that from a testator cannot be
lightly set on one side. Remember that,
Maud, when you weigh the matter in the
balances.'

Tor knew quite well that the more Maud
thought of a marriage with Lewis Belassis,
the less she would like it, so he had no misgivings about inculcating this dispassionate
consideration. He was doing the duty of an
elder brother, without any fear that his own
chances would suffer thereby. To be the dupe
of a Belassis plot and to be the victim of his
scheming would, he knew, be the more intoler-
able to her, the longer she looked at the
matter.

But Maud broke in upon his thoughts with
an imperious gesture.

' Nonsense, Phil ! I won't have you do anything romantic and ridiculous. This is a big
place, and you will want a lot of money to keep

it up. As long as you are not married, I'll live
here and keep house for you ; and when you
marry, I'll beg, borrow, or steal one of those dear
little cottages at the end of the park, and live
there on the remains of my fortune ; and you
shall keep a horse for me here, and ride out
with me once or twice a week ; and I'll stay
there an old maid, until somebody as nice as
you turns up and makes love to me, and then
I'll marry him. But,' and here she heaved a
melodramatic sigh, ' I'm afraid there is nobody
else in the world half as nice as you.'

' Of course not,' he answered, smiling. ' Now
sit down, Maud, and let us be sensible for once.
I do want to find out, if I can, why Mrs. Belassis
cribbed that paper. She must have had a
motive, and a strong one. She would not
have done anything quite so suspicious without.'

' That's true,' assented Maud; and she returned to a minute examination of the paper.

After turning it round and round several
times, she proceeded to unfold it, and then
her eyes opened wide with a look of comprehension.

' Look here, Phil ! She has been rubbing

something out. There was something written in pencil on the inside. What was it?'

Tor looked over her shoulder, and saw plain traces of careful erasure. He pulled at his moustache, and whistled under his breath.

' By Jove! So she has!'

' What was it, Phil?' asked Maud eagerly. ' What had old Uncle Maynard written there?'

' I don't know, Maud. I had never unfolded the paper. It never occurred to me that there was writing on the inside.'

' No,' said Maud slowly. ' I don't suppose it did. Men are never curious, and there isn't anything to make anyone turn over. I wonder what it was. Something important, of course, or Aunt Celia would not have troubled to run a risk for it.'

All three faces were grave. Tor felt that through an unconscious blunder of his, some distinct damage might have been done to Phil, though how or why he could not tell. It was not easy to see what harm could ensue from neglect of a few pencilled words—added quite as an after-thought to the letter ; but at the same time, Mrs. Belassis' conduct had made it

evident that importance did attach to them ;
and Tor was disturbed at this discovery.

It was useless, however, to try to conjecture
what the last message could have been, and
lamentations over the casualty were equally
purposeless.   Tor had some dim hope that he
might surprise the truth from one or other of
the Belassis' at some later date, but at present
silence was their only course.

Maud talked herself sleepy, and went to bed ;
Mrs. Lorraine was about to follow her example,
when Tor asked her to remain a little while
longer, as he had something of importance he
wished to say to her.

The gentle little widow looked half surprised
at this announcement, for nobody since her husband's death had ever cared to discuss matters
of importance with her ; but she assented
readily, and settled herself once more in her
chair.

'Well, dear boy ?'

' I want to ask you what you know about
Alfred Belassis—of his early life, I mean.
You have always lived in this neighbourhood,
have you not ? You know as much of the
family history as anyone.'

' Yes, I suppose I do; but I do not know anything of Alfred Belassis' early life. I never saw him until a few years before he married Celia.'

' Who were the Belassis'?—the seniors, I mean? Were they not very much below your family in social position?'

' Yes, I always thought so. I always wondered how Celia could make such a marriage, though we ought not to be proud I suppose; and Alfred Belassis had very good worldly prospects.'

' I want you to tell me how it all came about, so far as you know the story. Begin with the father. How did the intimacy between the families begin?'

' The father was James Belassis. He was a solicitor in the town of Darwen—where the coach stops, you know. He was a respectable kind of man, but not a gentleman. Nobody knew much about him until father—our father, I mean—found out that he was a very clever man of business, and gradually put all his affairs into his hands. Other people followed father's example, and Belassis soon found himself in very much improved circumstances, and on the high-road to wealth. He had been a careful, saving man always, and had made a fair amount of money before; and I can remember father saying one day, that he had a son whom he had educated almost like a gentleman, and who was, he fancied, rather wild.'

'When did all this take place?' asked Phil.

'I don't exactly know when father first employed Belassis. It must have been when I was quite a girl. But it was, I think, in 1843 that Alfred Belassis first appeared upon the scene.'

'What made him come?'

'His father sent for him. He was getting on so well that he wanted his son to come and take a share of the business, and learn enough to step into his shoes. Alfred had been in the office when quite young; but his father had indulged him, and it had ended by his going off to see the world, that he might be made into a gentleman.'

'The world must be congratulated on the gentleman it has turned out,' remarked Tor. 'Well, the young man came back in '43, did he?—to a sudden prospect of wealth and importance; and what then?'

'I have always thought it was at that time that James Belassis began to have hopes of making a good marriage for his son, and I believe he always had his eye upon one of our father's three daughters. We were not bad-looking girls, Maud, Celia, and I; but men—marriageable men—were scarce, and it was not to be wondered at if James Belassis should make such a plan. His son would be rich, and he had had a gentleman's education, and was not a match to be utterly despised in these parts; I think our father secretly favoured him. He wanted his daughters well married, I know.'

'Did Alfred Belassis fall in with his father's plans for his future?' asked Tor, in rather a peculiar tone.

'Yes, I think so. He came here often, and paid us all a good deal of attention; but for several years nothing happened. I think it was four years before he even proposed to Celia. Maud had married your father by that time, and I think it was soon afterwards that he asked Celia; and they were engaged quite a long time. I used to think he didn't really want to marry her—he kept putting it off so much.

Men were generally afraid of Celia; I think that was why she never had an offer till Alfred Belassis asked her. I don't think she ever cared very much for him; but father was for it, and she wished to be independent. I used often to fancy Alfred was half afraid of her. He was so very long in coming to the point.'

' When were they married ?'

' In May, 1850—I remember I did not like them to be married in May; but Celia said it was all superstitious nonsense. Alfred would have waited till June, but Celia said if it wasn't in May it should be in April; and then they settled for May. Celia had got quite out of patience with his " shilly-shallying." She threatened to break off the match, if he never intended to get married.'

' Why didn't he break it off, if he was so much afraid ?'

' Oh, he never could bear her to talk like that. He was bent on the marriage, but he seemed so inclined to keep putting it off. He acted very oddly altogether. You know Celia was a good match; for I was cut out of father's will when I married, and Maud and Celia had my fortune between them. Celia was father's favourite, and she got the most in the end.'

Tor sat still, digesting what he had heard. All pointed conclusively to the theory he had formed, that Alfred Belassis had not verified the fact of his first wife's death, before his marriage with Celia Maynard. He had evidently been summoned home suddenly, to hear of an increase of fortune, and fairly good worldly position, and the prospect of an excellent marriage; and he had not had the honesty or courage to confess that he was already married. A wife like Nelly Roberts would be a millstone round his neck all his life, preventing his ever rising to the standing he might otherwise hope to attain; and with his usual lack of principle, and clumsy cunning, he had trusted that chance would favour him, and that the ex-lady's-maid would remain in the seclusion where he had left her, and never trouble him more.

At the end of seven years he evidently had heard nothing of her, and had then, though obviously with some misgivings, entered a second time into the bonds of 'holy matrimony.'

'Why do you ask all these questions, Philip?' asked Mrs. Lorraine. 'What can it matter now, how or when all this happened? I know it was an evil day for all of us when Belassis entered our family; but why do you want to know the details?'

'I will tell you why, Aunt Olive. It is a disgraceful story enough, and I do not wish it to go further; but it will be safe with you; and I think one of the family should know it.'

Mrs. Lorraine looked half surprised, half alarmed.

'What is it, dear boy?'

'Did Belassis ever mention a former marriage to your sister, or to anyone?'

'A former marriage? Oh dear no! He was not married, and never could have been. He was only about three-and-twenty when he came here, and he lived here seven years before he married. Oh no, he could not have been married before that—it is quite impossible. What makes you ask such a very odd question?'

'Because he was married before—he made a low sort of marriage, with a pretty lady's-maid, only a few months before he appeared at Ladywell.'

And forthwith Tor launched into the history of his visit to Whitbury, and the discovery which had been forced upon him there.

Aunt Olive listened aghast, especially when it dawned upon her that her brother-in-law was a much greater rascal than even she had ever before believed, and that he had shamefully deceived her sister. Only too well did she now perceive the cause of his uneasiness before the wedding; and her dismay at the possibility, to which they could not blind themselves, fairly took her breath away.

'I trust all may be well on *that* score,' said Tor, knowing well what was in her mind. 'For the girl did die, poor thing, somewhere about 1850, and we shall try to ascertain the exact date if it is possible. I do not in the least believe that this disgraceful episode need ever be made public; but I think it will give me the whip-hand of Belassis if ever he is troublesome. The secret is known only to me and to Miss Marjory Descartes. I think we are both to be trusted. I shall do nothing which might bring down sorrow and disgrace upon the innocent. If he lets my affairs alone, I will let his.'

Tor was not long in finding that he had got the whip-hand of Belassis pretty considerably. He was riding over the farm the following day, when the uncle joined him, mounted on an old screw, which was too broken-down in spirit to frighten the most timid horseman.

' Ah, Phil, my boy !' he cried with great heartiness. ' Just the fellow I wanted to see. Ride on with me a little away from these clodhoppers—so, not too fast. I just wanted a word or so with you.'

' Certainly, sir.'

' Hum—ah—well—you spoke last evening of Whitbury, did you not ?'

' I believe I did, sir.'

' Ah, yes—well, perhaps you might have observed a little constraint in my manner, did you ?—a little absence of my usual frank heartiness—eh ?'

' I certainly did notice something odd. I fancied it might be a threatening of cholera,' answered Tor, ' you went so green.'

' Ha! ha! Very good—cholera indeed! What a wag you are, Philip ! No, no—now let us see—what was I saying? Oh, Whitbury? yes; and Miss Marjory Descartes. I suppose my name was not mentioned between you?'

'She seemed to know the name Belassis, when it came up casually in conversation. I believe she had known a Belassis in past days. A relation of yours?'

'Ah well, never mind now. I know you're not a chatterer, Philip, and I'm going to make a father confessor of you. Ha! ha! that's rather good, isn't it? I say, old chap, do you know what wild oats are?'

He dug Tor playfully in the ribs. The young man smiled, and answered readily:

'Well, yes, sir; I have some acquaintance with the article. They are generally pleasanter things to sow than to reap.'

'Why, yes, boy; so you have found that out too! Ah me! we all run a bit wild in our youth. I dare say you have played Don Juan sometimes before now—eh? Well, never mind that. It isn't fair to ask too many such questions. But to come to the point; what I want to tell you is this—I sowed most of my wild oats in Whitbury.'

' Indeed !'

' Yes, I did ; and that's why I didn't much care to talk about the place. Now mind you, boy, I did nothing really wrong—no, no. I was wild and foolish ; but I never disgraced my father's name '—here his face assumed an edifying expression of virtuous complacency. ' I was only a bit gay and wild ; but still one doesn't like such episodes brought to light after a number of years—you will know better what I mean when you are married, and settled down in life. My wife, now, is what I call a fastidious woman—an uncommonly particular, upright, conscientious woman.'

' Quite so,' ejaculated Tor softly.

' Eh ? yes, quite so ; I knew you would agree with me, and you can understand that I don't want old Whitbury gossip to come to her ears. I don't want to meet Miss Marjory Descartes, or for her to meet Celia. I'd rather she never came near the place at all. And I'll take it as a personal favour, Philip, if you will not talk about such things before my wife, or put ideas into her head, or have Miss Marjory to Ladywell at all.'

Belassis was flushed, breathless, and incoherent. Tor answered gravely enough:

'I can't promise not to ask Miss Marjory to Ladywell; but you can keep out of her way as much as you please. If I were you, I would tell your wife about these innocuous wild oats, and get the matter off your mind. However, I have no wish to introduce the subject. I always think people had much better not meddle with their neighbours' affairs.'

Even Belassis' thick head caught at the meaning of these last significant words.

'Oh, ah—yes,' he answered uneasily. 'I never do interfere—I don't mean to. We'll just keep on good terms, and let one another alone.'

Belassis rode off as rapidly as he dared, feeling unequal to prolonging the interview. Tor, who had seen Maud's hat over a distant hedge, put his horse to a gallop, and joined her by a flying leap.

'Phil! how you do startle one! What are you up to now?'

'I've been talking with our respected uncle. I don't think he'll bother us much more. The open defiance will hardly be needed.'

' You met Uncle Belassis ?'

' Yes ; I have just parted from him.'

' Was he riding ?'

' Well, I can hardly say that. He sat on his horse, and the horse ran.'

Maud laughed delightedly, and her mind was diverted from the question of the interview, as Tor intended it should be.

' Oh, Phil,' she said, ' there came a letter for you by the mid-day post. It's from Germany, and I think perhaps it's from Tor, or about him.'

Tor hastened home with all the speed he could, an eager hope possessing him that he might see at last Phil's familiar handwriting.

CHAPTER V.

A VISIT TO GERMANY.

BUT no, the letter was not from Phil ; but in the crabbed, minute writing of the German brain-doctor.

Tor opened the envelope with haste, and ran his eyes rapidly over its contents, a look of impatience and dismay crossing his face as he did so.

The letter was in German, and was somewhat floridly worded ; but its meaning was only too plain.

Phil was no better—was in fact worse; that is to say, the prolonged insensibility was an unfavourable sign. But Dr. Schneeberger was not despondent. On the contrary, he still held to his original statement that he believed time and patience would effect a cure ; but he strongly advocated a different method of treat-

ment.   He was, in fact, very anxious to send
his patient away on a sea voyage, feeling confident that the change; the sea air and easy
motion of the sailing vessel, would do him
much good.   A friend of his was just about
to start on a cruising expedition in the Pacific,
and had volunteered to take charge of ' Herr
Torwood.'   He was a medical man, a friend
of Dr. Schneeberger, who was going himself
for rest and change, and would be absent only
four months.   Four months might do wonders
for the patient, and he was most anxious that
the experiment should be tried.   Both doctors
were in its favour, and they only awaited
Mr. Debenham's consent.

Tor read the letter thoughtfully, and looked
at the case in all its bearings.   Just once the
doubt crossed his mind, whether it would not
be better to bring Phil home as he was, tell the
whole story, and let him await his recovery in
his own house, and in his rightful position ;
but a little thought decided him against
such a step.   Were Phil brought home in
that state, Mr. and Mrs. Belassis, as next
of kin, would have great power; and their
first step would doubtless be to prosecute

Tor for his 'felony and forgery.' Matters
had now gone too far for such a step to be
practicable, and the game had not grown
so desperate yet that Tor felt in any way
obliged to throw it up. Indeed, since his
late discoveries with regard to the rectitude of
both Mr. and Mrs. Belassis, he had felt
strengthened in his position, through the sense
of having his enemies to a certain extent in
his power.

On mature consideration, Tor decided that
it would be best to allow the experiment of the
sea voyage. Should it succeed, as the doctors
seemed convinced that it would, all would
be well; and if not, no risk was run, so far as
he could see, and matters would be in no worse
state than they were now. Meantime, it
might be rather a relief than otherwise to feel
that Phil was safely away at sea, because Mrs.
Belassis was certainly suspicious of something
—of what, Tor did not know ; and if by
chance her prying eyes discovered Dr. Schneeberger's address, and she took a fancy to visit
him and see his patient, there was no knowing
what unpleasant results might not ensue.

This idea had struck Tor when he realized

how his locks had been tampered with, and it was not a welcome thought. Mrs. Belassis was anything but a stupid woman; and once let her get a clue into her hands, she would pursue it relentlessly and sagaciously to the bitter end. Therefore, it might be no bad move to get Phil quickly and quietly out of her reach.

Tor therefore wrote his consent, but determined to see Phil and the doctor before the plan was put into execution ; and, to Maud's despair, announced that he was going to start for Germany at once.

' Oh, Phil !'

' Well, Maud, I thought you were so anxious for me to go and see Tor.'

' Are you going to see him ? Are you going to bring him here ?'

' The doctor recommends a sea voyage— you can see what he says if you can read his German hieroglyphics. I must go over and see about it.'

Maud tried to decipher the letter, but ended by bringing it across for Tor to translate. She looked half-pleased, half-disappointed to hear of the plan. Tor left out the piece where the

' prolonged insensibility ' was mentioned. He did not wish the nature of his friend's malady to be generally known. The reason for his reticence on this point was simply this. If Mrs. Belassis got hold of the right idea as regards Phil and his friend, and knew that one man was in a state of helpless torpor, it would at once be plain how easily a clever deception might be practised by the other. But if both were in possession of their senses, it was evident that what was done must be by mutual agreement ; and so long as this was the case, nobody but the man concerned had any right to interfere with the part his friend was playing.

' I wish he had suggested sending him to England instead. I believe English doctors could cure him.'

' Well, if this little fellow fails, we will employ the faculty here ; but I'm inclined to try this sea voyage first. The doctors speak with confidence, and one does not like to thwart them on such a point.'

' But why does he write to ask you ? Can't Mr. Torwood decide for himself ?'

' I'm afraid by this that he's not so well

26—2

again, and that he has referred them to me to judge for him. He always threw the management and responsibility of things upon me at the best of times. He is sure to do so more than ever now. I must certainly go over and see about it.'

So Tor went, and Maud was left alone; and in the afternoon, when she had seen him off upon the coach, she drove to the Merediths, and dismissed the carriage, so that she might spend some time with the blind man and his daughter.

Tor had been a little less frequent in his visits since the strange proposition on behalf of his daughter which Mr. Meredith had made to him about ten days before; and his journey to Yorkshire and this sudden call to Germany explained his absence most satisfactorily.

' Alone, Maud ?' said Mr. Meredith, as he heard the girl's step in the room. ' I thought you would have surely brought Philip with you to-day.'

' I have just taken Phil to the coach. He sent me to explain matters to you. Phil has to go to Germany to see his friend, who is ill. I'm afraid he will be gone a whole week.'

'Gone away again!' echoed Mr. Meredith, in a tone of disappointment. 'Why, we have not seen anything of him for five whole days!'

'He has been in Yorkshire, you know, on his friend's business, and only came back the night before last. Then, to-day came another letter, which sent him tearing off again. I'm afraid his friend is a sad plague to him just now—though, of course, he owes ever so much to him.'

'A good friend—a good brother,' said Michael Meredith, with his slow satisfied smile. 'Such a man will make a good husband, too —eh, Maud ?'

'Do you mean Phil, Uncle Michael ? Oh yes ; I should think he would make the best husband in the world. He is so good and kind and considerate to everyone. But I don't much fancy he means to get married— not yet, at any rate.'

'Ah, Maud, sisters are not always their brothers' confidantes on such subjects.'

Maud looked rather nettled.

'I'm sure Phil would tell me directly; he tells me everything about himself.'

'He is a wonderful brother, then,' said Meredith ; but his own face had clouded over somewhat, and by-and-by he asked, with a touch of sharpness in his tone :

'Has he never spoken to you, then, of his engagement ?'

'His engagement?'

'Yes ; are you so much astonished ? Did you not know that he was half-engaged?'

Maud calmed down a little after her first amazement. She knew that the blind man was given to romancing, but she could not yet understand the bearing of such a remark as this.

'No, Mr. Meredith. I don't know anything about it. To whom is he half-engaged ?'

'To Roma.'

This was said with an air of such pride and satisfaction that Maud nearly smiled. She wondered if it could be true. Phil had been to see the blind man and his daughter a great deal, and had of late seemed more interested in Roma ; but certainly Maud had seen no traces of anything like a romantic attachment.

'Phil engaged to Roma!' she repeated. 'He never said a word to me!'

'Well,' returned Meredith slowly, half-ready to retract what he had said, now that he had produced the desired effect, 'perhaps I should hardly say "engaged," because there has been no pledge asked or given on either side, as yet. I do not wish the quiet current of Roma's young life disturbed, and your brother can afford to wait. But words have passed between him and me ; I have read his inmost heart, and have found it loyal and true—as his father's was before him ; and now we understand one another, and he is prepared to abide by my wishes as to the time of probation.'

For by this time Michael Meredith had fully persuaded himself that the delay was of his own making, that the young man was eager and willing to come forward to claim Roma's hand, but that he withheld him, in order that his daughter's young heart should not be too early or too roughly awakened from its sleep of happy childhood. This Meredith fully believed, and Maud half-believed it too.

It was a good thing for Tor that Mr. Meredith had so deceived himself, as it had saved

him from any further allusions to a subject
not at all agreeable to him. Maud pondered
awhile over these words, and finally said :

'Is Roma so very young? I always
thought her so wise for her age.'

'Roma is twenty-five. She may be wise in
some things, I do not deny it; in others, she
is innocent as a child.'

'Is she?'

'Certainly. Have you not observed it for
yourself?' asked Meredith.

'I don't know. I have never thought
Roma at all childish.'

'She is a child in all matters that refer to
the heart,' said Michael Meredith, in his
sententious way. 'A child to love.'

'Well, but is it not time——' began Maud.

'Not yet—not yet,' answered Meredith,
anticipating her. 'I hold her sleeping heart
in my hand ; when I bid, it shall awaken.'

Maud considered this great nonsense. That
a girl of Roma's age should be treated so like
a child or a baby was manifestly absurd, and
she thought that Mr. Meredith was very
foolish and very wrong. If Phil wanted
Roma, he ought to be allowed to propose

sensibly, as other men did ; and be accepted or
refused, as they were. What was the use of
waiting ? Roma was surely old enough to
know her own mind.

Mr. Meredith was acute enough to read dis-
satisfaction in her silence, and a few questions
brought out the cause. Without the least
intention of doing any mischief, she infused
her own feelings into Mr. Meredith's mind,
and he began to wonder what was the use of
this delay, and to grow fretful and impatient.

Maud soothed him down, as she knew well
how to do ; but Michael Meredith was not
easily satisfied that day.

' You must go and talk to Roma,' he said.
' You said she would know her own mind by
this time, and would accept or refuse Philip.
She shall not refuse him—I will not have it.
Go and find out what she feels, and tell her I
will not have her do anything foolish. When
he asks her, she is to marry him ; I have made
up my mind, and she must not disappoint me.'

Maud went to seek Roma in her studio.
She had no fear that any sane person would
reject her idolized Phil ; and on the whole, she
was not sorry that he had turned his thoughts

in her direction. For Maud was sincerely fond of Roma.

She had constituted herself a kind of 'guide, philosopher and friend' to this lonely girl who led so secluded a life, and so seldom mingled in any kind of society. Maud's experiences were not very wide, nor her philosophy very deep; still she had a certain share of shrewd worldly wisdom, and a warm, affectionate nature; and Roma had fallen into the way of giving and receiving confidences when Maud came to see her, which would have been impossible to her with any other companion.

'Now, Roma,' began Maud, when preliminary matters had been disposed of, 'I have come to say something, and of course I shall go straight to the point at once. Is Phil in love with you?'

'No, certainly not.'

'Are you sure?' asked Maud archly.

'Perfectly sure,' answered Roma quietly.

Maud looked rather blank. Something in Roma's manner carried conviction with it.

'I suppose father has been talking to you,' she said. 'I wish he would not. It is one of his fancies, Maud, that your brother is to marry me ; but he never will. He does not care for me, nor I for him—in that way.'

' But your father said he had spoken about it—Phil, I mean.'

A look of pain crossed Roma's face.

' That means, I suppose, that father has spoken to Mr. Debenham—I wish he would not. Your brother is kind, and humours him because agitation is so bad for him. Please do not talk to me any more about it. It is a horrid state of affairs. But you may be quite sure that your brother and I will never marry.'

' Would you refuse him if he asked you ?'

' He never will ask me.'

' But suppose he did,' urged Maud. ' You know he might, Roma ; he likes you very much.'

The girl clasped her hands tightly together, with a look of keen pain upon her face.

' I suppose then, I should have to say yes, for my father's sake. I cannot—*cannot* go against him—not even to save my own life. Some day, Maud, I will try and tell you why. Oh! I hope and trust it may not be, for I must do my father's bidding.'

Maud was able to give Mr. Meredith the

required assurance, and to leave him in a state of placid tranquillity ; but she left the house in a dissatisfied frame of mind, and wished that she had never been there. She could not believe that Phil would be so weak as to let Mr. Meredith cajole him into a marriage that he was not anxious to make ; and it was very hard upon him to have to humour the old man because it was bad for him to be vexed. Altogether Maud felt annoyed and disturbed —vexed with herself for what she had said to Mr. Meredith, with him for being so foolish and irrational, and with Roma for talking and looking as though marriage with Phil would be the most dreadful thing in the world.

She thought things had come to an odd sort of pass, and determined that she would not go to the house again until Phil had come back, and could tell her the true state of the case. For in spite of all that Mr. Meredith had implied, she knew her brother would be frank with her.

Meantime Tor was travelling rapidly towards Freyburg, at which place he arrived one even-

ing, about twelve hours later than his letter
had done.

From the hotel he walked straight up to
Dr. Schneeberger's house, and was met by the
lively little Gretchen, who welcomed him with
volubility and warmth, and was genuinely
delighted to see him.

But she shook her head in mournful fashion
over the helpless state of his poor friend, and
lamented its sadness. Such a fine handsome young man—everyone said that who
saw the Herr Torwood. Ah, it was what
nobody could understand, that he should be
struck down like that.

Tor asked for the doctor, who quickly
appeared, looking just as dried up as ever,
but somewhat more anxious and constrained
in manner, from which Tor feared he had
formed an unfavourable opinion of his friend's
case. But he spoke more hopefully than
before, and seemed to have great confidence in
the sea voyage. He had taken other opinions,
and all had agreed that the experiment should
be tried. Once or twice he had fancied he
detected some faint return of mental power,
but it had never lasted. Still there seemed

some probability that the change of air, the movement and the stir, might awaken the dormant faculties.

The little doctor talked rapidly and energetically, and Tor quietly acquiesced in all he said. Then he asked to see his friend, and was taken up to the little clean, bare room that he so well remembered, and which he could fancy he had only quitted yesterday.

Phil lay upon the bed, just as he had done before, his eyes closed, his breath coming somewhat heavily through the parted lips. His hair and beard had grown, and were wild and tangled. Tor was almost glad that the sheet half-concealed the lower part of the face. The brow and eyes and upper part belonged to the familiar face of his chosen friend and companion. Those were Phil's well-known, well-cut features. He did not care to look below, where the changes induced by illness had given an air of neglect to the once carefully trimmed moustache and smooth-shaven cheeks.

He looked down upon the unconscious face before him with an honest, manly compassion.

'Poor old fellow! Poor old—Tor!' he

muttered (the little doctor stood opposite looking at him, so he must not trip, even in English).

'Well, mein Herr,' said the doctor, 'what think you of your friend?'

'I don't know what to think. He looks just the same to me. I suppose it's no good my speaking to him? He wouldn't hear?'

'You can try,' answered Dr. Schneeberger with a dim interest in his tone.

'If only he would go!' thought Tor, but he could not suggest this, and it sounded a mockery to address the unconscious Phil by a false name. Still, he bent over him, and called rather loudly:

'Tor! Torwood! wake up, old fellow! Don't you know me—Phil Debenham? Tor, I say!'

Perhaps there was the faintest motion of the eyelashes—neither Tor nor the doctor could be certain; but the eyes remained fast closed, and no other words evoked the slightest sign of life.

Tor gave one last long look, and turned away with a sigh. He almost wished he had never come. It was so melancholy to see the friend lie there helpless and vacant, whose help he needed so much.

That evening was spent in consultation with the doctor, and on the morrow Tor left for England again. He would gladly have been Phil's travelling companion upon this voyage, but affairs at Ladywell would not permit of his prolonged absence. So he had to leave Phil in the care of the kindly Germans, who gave him many hopeful assurances, that when next he saw his friend he would be restored to health and strength.

Tor sincerely hoped that they would prove right.

CHAPTER VI.

DISCOMFITED.

WHEN Belassis heard that his trouble-some nephew had gone to Germany, and would probably be absent for a week, he seemed to breathe more freely again ; for since the evening on which he had heard of the sudden visit to Whitbury, he had felt like one who lives with a drawn sword suspended over his head. Not even his con-versation in the field on the following day had restored his shaken equanimity, for he was not at all assured that his statement had been believed, although it had not been contradicted. Belassis and his wife had both ample food for meditation, and were glad of the respite which this visit to Germany had afforded.

'Now is our time, if ever, to search for the will,' said Mrs. Belassis, the same evening that

Lewis had told them of the sudden journey. 'Why did we not have this clue before, when Ladywell stood empty? We could have done anything then. Now it may be difficult, and even dangerous.'

Belassis shook his head helplessly, and did not know what to suggest.

'You never do,' returned his wife coolly. 'I can't think what has come to you, Alfred; you used to have plenty of assurance, and meddled with matters you had much better have let alone, and now that a real emergency has come, you are no better than a girl. I'd be ashamed to be such a poor creature.'

Belassis did not resent this language, for he felt himself a poor creature enough at that moment. What his wife said of him was only too true. Some change had come over him for which he could not account, and his old cunning and craft seemed to have entirely deserted him.

As a fact, it was circumstances that had changed, not his nature. Belassis was a man who could go on swimmingly whilst things were prosperous, whilst the game was in his own hands, and success within his grasp, but he could not stand up against misfortune ; and when the tide of his luck seemed turning, he could only look on dismayed, feeling hopelessly unequal to the task of stemming the torrent.

His father had been a clever man, and had put his son in the way of becoming wealthy and respected. He left him a handsome property and a flourishing business, and had secured for him a well-dowered wife. Alfred Belassis therefore had made an excellent start in life, for he was trusted and respected for his father's sake, and admitted into society for his wife's.

So long as he had only had to deal with men like Philip Debenham senior, all had gone well. He had fleeced him with impunity, speculated with his money, and had contrived that all gain should be his own, and all loss his client's. He had even gone so far as to speculate with Maud's trust-money, and the speculation had been a lamentable failure.

Belassis' own fortune, too, had suffered through his folly and ill luck ; and since this new relative had turned up, with his cool inquiring words and amused incredulous looks, the ground seemed actually slipping away from under his feet, and he could only lean upon his wife for support. The idea that she might now learn the treacherous part he had played towards her, was an added terror; and Belassis sometimes felt disposed to make a bolt for it, and get away altogether from his present surroundings, but his natural weakness and irresolution deterred him.

'I'm afraid I am but a poor creature, my dear,' he answered, with a sickly smile. 'I think I cannot be very well just now.'

'Pooh, nonsense! You're well enough, only cowardly. Now look here. I'm nearly sure that Philip Debenham has never seen those words about the later will. For one thing, I don't believe the paper had ever been unfolded before I opened it out; and for another, if Philip had known of it, the search would have been instituted at once; and if the will had been in existence at all, it would have been found. I've never heard that any search has been made; and besides, although Philip did ask you something about a later will, it seemed to be pure guess-work, for he imagined that it had fallen into your hands.'

'I wish to heaven it had!' groaned Belassis.

'If there is another will, and if it is found, we shall be ruined.'

'Just so ; and as we both believe that another will was made, we must take care that it falls into no hands but our own.'

Belassis groaned again.

'You really think he made another ?'

'You know I always did think he intended making another, when you told me how perfectly ready he was to agree to your suggestion, and to make that condition, and write that letter. You had plenty of bluster in those days, Alfred, and Philip feared you; and you could always get the whip-hand of him by threatening to throw up his business affairs, which he was fool enough to think were prospering in your hands. He dared not oppose you ; but I never trusted him, when I knew how easily he had granted that monstrous condition, and that without any love for us or for Lewis. If he had argued and disputed and then given way, I might have believed better in it ; as it was, I never had much faith.'

'Nor I very much ; but I never could find out anything suspicious, and I watched him as a cat does a mouse. Nothing in his papers was found to upset the will in my possession.'

'Well, there can be no doubt now that the will was made ; the only question is, was it accidentally or purposely destroyed ? or is it still in the library at Ladywell, hidden away ? As Philip Debenham had the acuteness to put it somewhere out of your reach, it is hardly likely he would ever be weak enough to make away with it himself. I believe it is still there.'

Belassis wiped his forehead with his handkerchief.

'Old Maynard could not find it.'

'Old Maynard would not look with the energy that we shall. If it is there, find it we *must.*'

'How ?' asked Belassis vaguely.

'That remains to be proved. After what has gone before, it may be difficult ; but I will make an attempt whilst Philip is away ; if that fails, we must consider further.'

Mrs. Belassis did make the attempt without further loss of time. That same afternoon she went over to Ladywell, in order to consult some books of reference in the library.

She had done the same thing sometimes in the former owner's time, as a means of gaining occasional access to her gruff old uncle. In this lay her chief hope, that her visit might pass unremarked, and that she might be allowed to prosecute her search unsuspected.

The library at Ladywell was of great size, and contained a really large collection of books. If the will was concealed in one of these, it might be a weary while before it saw the light. Still Mrs. Belassis was not daunted by that thought. If it was there, she would find it, if only opportunity were granted her. The strong probability that, even if in existence, it might lie undiscovered for generations, was but a poor consolation to Mrs. Belassis. So long as she believed it to be there, she could enjoy no rest. Any day some chance might reveal its hiding-place, and then ruin stared them in the face. It must be found by herself or her husband, and destroyed as soon as found, and then perhaps they would know peace again.

So Mrs. Belassis went openly to Ladywell, and was shown by her own request into the library. Miss Debenham and Mrs. Lorraine,

she was told, were to start in ten minutes'
time for a garden-party.

This was good news. Mrs. Belassis took
down a few books, and sat down to study
them, to give colour to her story in case either
lady should come in. It was not many
minutes before Maud entered. Her cheeks
were flushed, and her eyes sparkled a little as
she addressed Mrs. Belassis.

' Oh, Aunt Celia, I heard you were here.
I am afraid you will be disappointed if you
stay. I don't think Phil keeps any of his
private papers in the library. Would you not
like to go up to his bedroom ? I do not know,
of course, as I am not specially interested in
his correspondence ; but I dare say you would
find there a good deal you might like to see.'

Mrs. Belassis looked coldly contemptuous.
Inwardly she was raging.

' Such a remark hardly deserves an answer,
Maud.'

' What a good thing, for I am afraid you
would not find it very easy to make one,'
retorted Maud quickly. ' Well, I must go
now. I hope you will find the books interesting, but I am afraid you will be disappointed.'

Maud swept away, and Mrs. Belassis heaved a sigh of relief. She believed that she would not now be further molested ; and when she heard the carriage roll away, a smile of triumph crossed her face. The triumph was short-lived. The door opened softly and admitted Mrs. Lorraine.

' Good-afternoon, Celia. I have brought my work in here this afternoon. It is the coolest room in the house, I think.'

She sat down beside the window, and drew out her work, talking quietly and gently the while.

' I thought you were going to a party with Maud,' said Mrs. Belassis sharply.

' I have changed my mind. It is too hot to enjoy such things.'

' You have never let Maud go alone ! She is not to be trusted by herself anywhere.'

' I have the greatest confidence in dear Maud. But she will not go alone. We were to call for Mrs. Nelson. Maud will go now under her care.'

Mrs. Belassis turned over her books with the haste of deeply-seated annoyance. Then she turned irritably upon the gentle sister, whom she had been accustomed for so many years to tyrannize over successfully.

'Well, I wish you would go away now, Olive. I can't bear company when I want to study.'

'I will not disturb you,' answered Mrs. Lorraine, settling herself quietly back in her chair.

Mrs. Belassis looked rather as she might have done had a dove turned upon her.

'You decline to leave me, do you, Olive?'

'Yes, Celia, I do. You are our guest whilst you are in this house—Maud's and mine. It is not usual to leave guests alone.'

Mrs. Lorraine spoke timidly yet firmly. She had not lived two months under Tor's protection for nothing. She was not ashamed or afraid to assume that position which he had always accorded to her. But Mrs. Belassis' wrath knew no bounds, and to Olive she allowed it to burst out.

'In point of fact, you have remained behind in order to spy upon my doings?'

'And whose fault is it if I have?' asked Mrs. Lorraine, not without dignity. 'What should we have seen had anyone spied upon

you whilst you were shut up in Philip's room
the other day? It is you who force us to
watch you, Celia. Philip is away, and we are
responsible for what goes on in his absence.'

Mrs. Belassis sneered.

'And so I cannot be allowed to make a few
notes from these books without supervision?
Even old Uncle Maynard, the misanthrope,
was less cautious than you seem to be. Are
you afraid that I shall walk off with some rare
book? I cannot think what has come over
you, Olive.'

'I could say the same of you, Celia. Why
should you object to my presence here,
unless——'

But Mrs. Belassis rose with dignity.

'I shall not remain here to be insulted.
Some day, Olive Lorraine, you shall be made
to rue the day when you played the spy upon
me, and made me Philip Debenham's declared
enemy.'

'I think enmity is better declared than
secret, Celia,' answered Mrs. Lorraine tranquilly. 'You have always been Philip's
enemy, and you know it.'

'And now you shall learn what my enmity

is like, and how it can affect your idolized nephew. Tell him to look to himself !'

And Mrs. Belassis, with a vindictive scowl at her daring sister, turned and quitted the room and the house, feeling for once that she was foiled.

Lewis had gone to the garden-party whither Maud was bound ; and he had gone thither with the fixed intention of having some serious conversation with her. This intention was partly the result of his own impatience, and his desire to come to some more definite understanding with his pretty cousin, and partly on account of a conversation he had had with his father upon the previous evening, in which Belassis had urged upon him with much force and feeling, the absolute necessity there was for him to marry Maud ; and had begged that he would not lose the opportunity afforded by the brother's absence. He felt certain that Maud would be more easily influenced in Philip's absence than if he were upon the spot; and he implored his son with feverish energy to lose no time, and to risk everything rather than let his cousin throw him over.

His father's excited manner left an uneasy

impression upon Lewis's mind. He could not see why it should be a life-and-death matter to anyone but himself, and yet there was no mistaking the eagerness of the elder Belassis. Lewis knew enough of his father to make him distrustful of such earnestness.

At the same time he was willing enough to talk to Maud, for he feared now that she was slipping from him, and he was determined not to yield her up without a struggle.

Poor Lewis! He felt sometimes as though he had deserved a better parentage and better prospects. He had been brought up in gentlemanly idleness, to satisfy his father's idea of grandeur and his mother's family pride, and was always considered a very lucky fellow, who would marry an heiress, or at least inherit her fortune, and succeed at length to the broad acres attached to Thornton House. But of late an uncomfortable idea had suggested itself to Lewis, that things were not quite so satisfactory as he had believed. His father's manner often perplexed him. His mother looked gloomy and disturbed, and he could not but fancy that some danger, unknown to him, threatened them at this time.

So it was in a rather dejected frame of mind that Lewis met Maud that afternoon, and dejection is not the most favourable of moods in which to commence a love-passage.

Maud was looking unusually bright and animated, and was always the centre of an admiring circle. It was some time before Lewis could gain possession of her, even for a few minutes, and not until quite the close of the afternoon that he succeeded in leading her away to a more secluded spot, beyond the reach of curious eyes or sharp ears.

' Why, Lewis, where are you taking me to ?' asked Maud, pausing at length and looking back. ' See what a long way we have wandered !'

' Yes, and see how nice and cool it is here !' returned Lewis. ' I'm sure you like it better than all that heat and glare. There's such a pretty little grotto down here by the water. You'd better come and see it, now you are so near.'

' Oh yes, I'll come. It's a pretty sort of place. It's been a nice party, hasn't it, Lewis ?'

'I hate tennis-parties!' answered he, with needless emphasis.

'Then why did you come?'

'I came to see you.'

'To see me!' Maud looked at him and laughed. 'That's good! As if you didn't see me nearly every day of your life!'

'I never seem to see you alone now for a moment,' returned Lewis discontentedly. 'You always have a crowd of people round you, or that everlasting Philip. I never can get in a word edgeways!'

Maud looked at him, and patted his arm gently with her delicately gloved hand.

'Now don't be silly and tiresome, Lewis. You know you haven't any real grievance. Is this the grotto? It is very pretty. Shall we sit down here a little while? Now you can talk to your heart's content.'

They did sit down, but at the same time Lewis did not seem to have very much to say. He looked at Maud, and looked at the trickling water, and held his peace. He had got the chance he wanted, but he did not seem to know how to use it.

Maud, too, was silent—and if not embarrassed, at any rate less ready than usual to chatter to him. She sat with a look of gravity stamped upon her face, which deepened as moments went by.

'Well, Maud,' said Lewis, looking up at length, 'I suppose we are both of us thinking about the same subject.'

'I dare say we are,' answered the girl slowly. 'I suppose it is time we came to some understanding, Lewis.'

It was not a very promising opening, and Lewis was aware of it.

'Well, Maud,' he said with a sigh, ' you know I have loved you all these years, and wanted to make you my wife. The question is, will you have me ?'

Had Maud's feelings been in any way likely to warm towards him, such a beginning would have been fatal ; but as it was, it did not affect the point at issue, because her mind was already made up.

'No, Lewis ; I'm afraid I can't, after all,' she said slowly. 'I do like you, and we've been very good friends always, and I've tried to make up my mind to it. I've looked at the matter every way, and considered everything, and I'm sure it would be best for us not to marry.'

Lewis sat looking gloomily at his boots.

'Aren't you fond of me, Maud, after the way we have held together all these years ?'

'Yes, Lewis, I am fond of you, and you are fond of me ; but I don't love you, and what's more, you don't love me—not in the way you think you do. I am sure we should not be really happy together, so you had better take the money, and leave me alone.'

'I don't want the money—I want you. It s a beastly shame the money ever was left like that.'

'Yes, so it is,' assented Maud readily ; 'but I can almost be glad that you will have it, Lewis, for you will find it very convenient. And—and I hope you won't go right away, or do anything rash ; because I'm very fond of you, Lewis, though I can't marry you.'

Maud spoke with sudden affection, and Lewis took the little hand she held out and kissed it.

'Why can't you marry me, Maud ? Once you thought you could. Do you care for any other fellow ?'

' No, no, Lewis ; indeed it isn't that.

' Then what is it ?'

'It is partly because I don't really care enough for you, Lewis ; and I don't think you would like to find that out after we were married ; and partly—partly because I do so detest Uncle Belassis and Aunt Celia. I could not—oh, I *could* not take their name, and make myself more of a relation than I am.'

' Rather hard on me,' remarked Lewis.

'Very hard on you,' assented Maud, with emphasis. 'I know it is, Lewis, and I feel almost mean to serve you so. Perhaps if I were in love with you, I could put up with even that ; but I'm not, and I really can't do it, more especially as I believe that clause in the will was all your father's doing—just a plot to keep the money in his own family. I think it's very hard on you to have such a father.'

Lewis shook his head gravely.

' I'm afraid sometimes he'll get into trouble one of these days. I believe he's been speculating awfully, and that plays old Harry with the money. I dare say I shan't be much of a catch after all, Maud. Perhaps you're wise to chuck me over.'

'Now don't be disagreeable, Lewis,' said Maud. 'You know if I wanted money, I should get it by marrying you. I'm glad you will have something substantial, even if Uncle Belassis does come to grief. I have thought him looking very anxious and frightened of late. Do you think anything has happened ?'

'I don't know. I fancy he has something on his mind, and the mater too. They will be in an awful way when I tell them your decision. I suppose you can't change it, Maud ?'

'I'm afraid not, Lewis ; I would if I could. But don't you tell them my decision. I will do that myself on my birthday. I will not give my final answer yet; I reserve to myself the right of changing my mind. Don't build on hope, but don't tell them anything. I should like to tell them myself.'

Lewis accepted this suggestion with some relief. He was cast down in spirit, and had no wish to face a blustering or craven father. He had taken his rejection more quietly than he had planned, because he saw at once from Maud's manner that his case was hopeless. For some reasons he felt this final decision

28—2

almost a relief. Maud had not been far wrong
in saying that his love was not of quite the
right kind ; and he was conscious that his
position as Maud's husband would be anything
but a pleasant one, did his father prove—as he
almost feared he would prove—to have committed follies, and even worse, which would
bring his name into unenviable notoriety. Lewis
had begun to have strong suspicions as to his
father's integrity, and these painful doubts had
been doubly painful when he had thought of
Maud.   He loved her well enough to wish to
spare her all needless pain—well enough to be
almost disinterested.   But this is hardly the
feeling of the ardent lover, and Maud was not
wrong in saying to herself that night, that the
interview was well over, and Lewis's heart was
not broken.

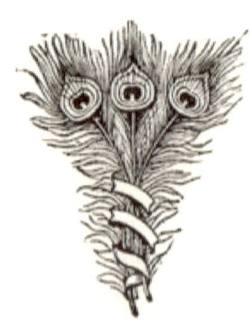

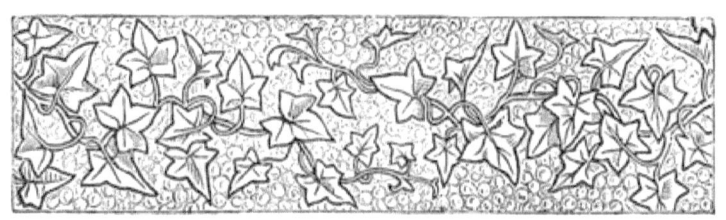

CHAPTER VII.

BETSY LONG.

MRS. BELASSIS had been discomfited by her sister and her niece—by the two beings she had been accustomed to snub and trample upon at will—and her defeat at their hands was as bitter a pill as she had ever been called upon to swallow.

Moreover, she was conscious of having brought her defeat upon herself by acting with less than her ordinary caution. What had occurred at Ladywell only a few days back, ought to have been enough to deter her from a second attempt at search. She had known this all along, but her intense eagerness to gain possession of the document, of whose existence they now felt certain, and the discovery of which, if made by other hands, would cause such a terrible *bouleversement* of all their cherished plans, had overcome her prudence.

With such a consummation staring her in the face, it was no wonder that Mrs. Belassis was willing to run some risk ; but now she wished she had been more circumspect. She felt she had put herself at a disadvantage by this second visit—had laid herself open to suspicion and contempt ; and a fear arose in her mind that, by showing her hand too openly, she might have given a clue to others as to the object of her search.

A little consideration, however, blunted the edge of this fear. If that letter of old Maynard's had not (as she felt certain) been opened out by other hands than hers, no one would ever dream of hunting for Philip Debenham's last will and testament amongst the wilderness of books in the library at Ladywell, which house had never been his home. If any-one believed that a second will had been made, they must also believe that it had been destroyed before now. It was not likely to come to light eighteen years after the death of the testator.

Whatever Maud and Mrs. Lorraine believed

that she (Celia Belassis) came to search for, they at least would never guess that it was for her brother-in-law's will. Of that fear she might safely rid her mind.

But she could not rid her mind of others. She knew that Roma Meredith came often now to read in the great library, and any day her unconscious choice might light upon the volume in which the precious paper lay hidden. Philip was himself something of a reader and a lover of books, and she had already heard some talk about rearranging the library and classifying the works.

Such thoughts as these made her blood run cold, and very earnestly and intently did she ponder over the matter, trying to see some way to rid herself of the haunting dread that oppressed her. She knew Maud's trust-money was all speculated away, and if anything occurred which should oblige her husband to deliver up the lump sum, it would be impossible to avoid a *fiasco* that must bring the name of Belassis into open contempt.

What Mrs. Belassis would like best to do, would be to carry war into the enemy's quarters, if only she saw her way to doing it.

She had not at all given up her idea that this
nephew of hers was playing a double part,
and acting unfairly towards the friend to
whom he owed so much. Her own eyes had
convinced her that he was using the money of
his friend as freely as his own ; and if he could
do that, of what was he not capable ?

She meant to keep her eyes and ears open,
and glean all the information possible upon
this subject. But it was not easy for her to
make discoveries now, because she had declared
open war, as it were, with those at Ladywell,
and was herself looked upon as little better
than a spy.

A spy !

Mrs. Belassis repeated the word once or
twice to herself, and an unpleasant smile stole
gradually into her eyes.

Yes, there was certainly something attractive in the idea. Would it be possible to
introduce a spy into that house, who would
keep watch upon what was going on, listen
and report upon all the talk of the servants'-
hall, and when it was possible, contrive to
hear what was said upstairs as well as down ?
Mrs. Belassis had a shrewd notion that ser-

vants generally contrived to find out the truth as to what went on in a house, much more quickly than they were supposed to do; and she believed that if her nephew was likely to get himself into trouble, he would probably tell something of his difficulties to his sister or his aunt, and then the secret would ooze out below-stairs, and might be easily made known to her. She thought she could perhaps set some rumour afloat herself, which might startle him from his high and mighty ease, and induce him to make some admissions to his two adoring relatives.

And again, if Mrs. Belassis could but introduce into that house some creature of her own, great things might be accomplished. The library books might be gradually and systematically examined; and if the underling failed in the quest, surely she could admit her employer at some unlikely hour, and with time and patience Mrs. Belassis felt perfectly certain that she should be able to find Philip Deben-ham's carefully hidden will.

But who was to be the instrument of this promising plot? A little more consideration, and that point, too, was settled.

When Mrs. Belassis reached her own house, she said to the footman who answered her summons:

'Send Betsy Long up to my room.'

Her face and voice were so severe, that the man informed the under-housemaid that 'she was going to catch it now, and serve her right too,' by which it might be argued that the young woman was not a special favourite of his.

Betsy Long was a good-looking, clever girl, and Mrs. Belassis had already made use of her as a sort of spy upon the other servants. It was her pride and boast, that she always knew exactly what went on in her kitchen and servants'-hall, and naturally this knowledge could only be obtained through one of the servants themselves. The honourable position of informer-general had been held for nearly two years by Betsy Long, who stood high in her mistress's favour, and proportionately low in that of her fellow-servants. Betsy Long could lie with an assumption of simple veracity that was touching to witness, and she knew when to speak and when to hold her peace; and she had always been faithful, so far, to her mistress, whom she feared whilst she fawned upon her. So Betsy Long was selected by Mrs. Belassis as her chosen instrument.

Betsy came up in fear and trembling, not knowing what might be in store for her. She was, however, somewhat reassured by the look and manner of her mistress; and the two entered into a long and earnest conference, the result of which will be seen later. The immediate result was, that the girl went sobbing down to the lower regions, with the news that Mrs. Belassis had turned her off with a week's notice, and she didn't know what would become of her.

The other servants could hardly be said to be sympathetic, and told her plainly that it served her right.

Betsy cried loudly in public, but never in private; and in spite of her mistress's supposed displeasure, she and Mrs. Belassis held, in strict privacy, more than one long conference together.

Mrs. Belassis felt easier in her mind now, as to matters connected with Ladywell; but she was not easy about the secret she believed her husband was hiding from her. She had so little faith in his acuteness, that she was convinced he might get into some very unpleasant mess, if he did not take her into his confidence. She was angry with him for his folly and recklessness in plunging himself into difficulties from which he seemed unable to extricate himself, and felt aggrieved to have another burden added to the load she was already forced to carry; but at the same time she was not going to stand by and let that stupid husband of hers keep an important secret from her.

'Alfred,' she said sharply, upon the first favourable opportunity, 'I asked you once before what you knew of Whitbury and Miss Marjory Descartes. You were pleased then to make a very ungentlemanly reply; perhaps now you will answer me properly.'

Belassis looked thoroughly frightened and taken aback.

'Wh—what do you kn—know about Wh—Whitbury?' he stammered, his face growing pale.

'I don't know anything yet; but I mean to know all pretty soon,' answered Mrs. Belassis coolly and firmly. 'You are not such a fool

as to try and deceive me? You ought to know
by this time that you couldn't do it.'

'Why should I know anything of Whitbury?' asked Belassis, trying all he knew to
speak naturally.

'Why should you turn perfectly livid at
the bare mention of the name, if you didn't?'

'I wasn't very well that evening—Philip
had startled me by coming in so suddenly
upon us.'

'Look here, Alfred!' said Mrs. Belassis
significantly. 'You know, and what's more, I
believe Philip Debenham knows, that you have
some mysterious connection with Whitbury.
If you won't tell me, I shall ask him; and if
he doesn't satisfy me, I shall apply direct to
Miss Marjory Descartes. I have not any
reason to suppose that she will screen you, if
she knows of anything to your discredit.'

Belassis thus brought to bay, collapsed suddenly and hopelessly. In encounters with his
wife he invariably got the worst of it.

'I—I— Indeed, my dear, I should have
told you all long ago, only it seemed useless
to rake up old stories of dead-and-gone follies.
Young men will be young men, you know;

and boys will be boys. I was little more than
a boy when I went to Whitbury to fish, and I
did get into some little trouble there—money
trouble, I mean—and I dare say if people hadn't
been good-natured, and not been too hard upon
me, it would have gone rather hardly with
me.'

Belassis, with an air of great good faith,
gave the particulars of the little fraud he had
unsuccessfully perpetrated (to which Miss Marjory had alluded in talking to Tor), and the
names given, and the circumstantial correctness
of the story, convinced Mrs. Belassis that it was
a true one.

'And why did Miss Marjory Descartes
stand your friend and beg you off?' she
asked.

'Because—because—— Well, my dear, the
truth is, I believe, a favourite maid of hers
begged her to do so, and interceded successfully with her. You see, I—I——'

'You had made love to the girl, I suppose?'
put in Mrs. Belassis scornfully. 'Just like
one of your low ways.'

'I had not seen you, you know, my dear;
and the girl was good-looking, and would

keep walking by the river in an evening, just where I was fishing. Of course I paid her a few compliments on her pretty face, and talked a little nonsense, as other young men do in similar circumstances. You needn't mind that, Celia, my love! I never looked at another woman after I knew you!'

Mrs. Belassis sneered.

' Do you suppose I am jealous of attentions you paid to a lady's-maid thirty or forty years ago? Was it fear of my displeasure that so alarmed you? or have you worse to tell?'

' Worse? Oh no!—no—no! That is all; the matter began and ended there. You know all I know now. You see, my dear, one does not care to have one's youthful sins and follies brought to light after all these years. I dare say it seems foolish to you; but I am fond of you, and I didn't care that a story like that—exaggerated and made worse, no doubt, by gossiping tongues—should come to your ears. I shall not mind, now that I have told you all; but, I confess, I was taken aback when Philip first spoke of Whitbury, and people I had known there. I did not know what ill-natured report he might not set afloat. Put yourself in my position a moment, my dear, and I think you will understand.'

'Well, well,' answered Mrs. Belassis impatiently, 'it is a pity, as you are such a poor cowardly creature, that you ever had courage to put yourself in such awkward positions as you have been doing of late. You can do a most daring and unscrupulous thing in the calmest way, so long as detection seems impossible; but as soon as ever the inevitable crisis threatens, you are as helpless and blundering as a child.'

Belassis assented to this criticism meekly enough, and took a good scolding from his wife with unusual docility. He was so unutterably relieved at the credence his story had obtained, that nothing else disturbed him much. Mrs. Belassis had certainly accepted his explanation with all readiness. His nature was so craven in her eyes that his fear was easily accounted for; and even she was far from suspecting him of the terrible and irretrievable folly of which he had really been guilty. That he would marry a second wife without knowing that the first was dead, was a thought that never crossed her mind for a moment. She never even suspected that he had ever been married, until his union with herself.

Days glided quietly by, and the traveller returned from his brief visit to Germany. He did not bring his friend back with him, as had been half expected in some quarters; but he announced that Mr. Torwood had started on a four months' sea-voyage, and was confidently expected to return from it with much recruited health.

Mrs. Belassis smiled a peculiar smile on hearing this announcement, and remarked that she had quite expected some such step as this—anything to keep his friend away. Her own theory on the subject was distinctly strengthened.

On the second day after his return, as Tor was sauntering leisurely homewards through the shady lanes, he came across a respectable-looking girl, sitting by the roadside and crying bitterly and uncontrollably.

He was too kind-hearted to pass by altogether unheeding, so he stopped, and asked the girl what was the matter.

With a great many sobs, and tears, and repetitions, the story came out.

She was, or had been, a housemaid at Thornton House for nearly two years, and her name was Betsy Long, and she was afraid she had a quick temper and a saucy tongue. The mistress had spoken about it more than once, and she had tried ; but some things would make a saint fly out—and to try and take away a poor girl's character !

Recalled to the point, she went on to say that Mrs. Belassis had missed some money off her dressing-table, and had accused Betsy of having taken it. The girl had denied it strenuously, and had lost her temper, and had become violent. Mrs. Belassis had discharged her at a week's notice, and had declined to give her a character ; and then Betsy, with a burst of sobs, explained that she had a mother and sick sister more than half dependent upon her, and that it would break their hearts to hear that she had lost her place without the chance of getting another ; for her character was gone, and she didn't know what would become of her.

There was sufficient sincerity in the girl's

manner to impress Tor with the belief that she was speaking the truth, and was innocent of the misdeed of which she had been accused. He was sorry for her, and thought that Mrs. Belassis had been hard, as might, perhaps, be expected from so hard a woman.

' I will speak to Mrs. Belassis for you,' he said, after a little reflection. ' You had better not give way like that. Come up to the Manor House this afternoon at five. We will see if something cannot be done for you.'

' Thank you, sir—thank you kindly,' said Betsy, with a curtsey, drying her eyes.

Tor was not far from Thornton House, so he turned his steps in that direction, and, at a corner, encountered Mrs. Belassis, bound for her own abode.

He lifted his hat and joined her, with a few words of greeting.

' I have just met your housemaid in great trouble at being summarily dismissed from your service. Has she really been robbing you ?'

' No ; I found out that my husband had taken the money, unknown to me, and I shall let Betsy know ; but at the same time she is such a saucy, impudent girl, I am quite glad to be rid of her.'

' You will not take her back, then ?'

'Certainly not, after such language as she used.'

' Had she not some excuse ? It was a serious charge against her. A little heat was only natural.'

' Then she must abide by the consequences. I will have nothing more to do with her. I can't bear the girl. I never could.'

' Will you give her a character ?'

' I shall see about it. I'll give her one for impudence if she applies.'

' Don't you think you're hard upon her ? She says she has relatives partly dependent upon her.'

' A mother and a sick sister, I believe she has ; but I don't see that that's any business of mine.'

' Have you found her a good servant in other ways ? Is she truthful ? Does she work well ?'

' I think those brazen-faced girls do speak the truth—they have no shame about anything. People say that bad-tempered servants do most work, and I cannot complain of Betsy upon that score ; but I can't imagine what earthly reason you can have for taking up her cause.'

' I am not aware that I am taking up any-one's cause. I merely want to know a few facts. Betsy Long is a good servant, with a bad temper ; is not that about the state of the case ?'

' I don't know your idea of a good servant ; mine is that she should know how to keep her place. If you're trying to trap me into saying I'll have Betsy back again, you'd better save your breath, for nothing would induce me to do it. Are you satisfied now ?'

' Perfectly so, thank you ; and I will now wish you good-morning.'

Mrs. Belassis smiled as she walked up the drive to her own door.

' I think he has taken the bait,' she said to herself. ' Men are so soft.'

Tor could hardly be said to be soft. He did not give any special heed to this incident of the forlorn Betsy ; but he felt sufficient indignation at Mrs. Belassis' hardness, and compassion for the girl's distress, to be wishful to do something to place her in a better position.

He told Maud and Aunt Olive what had occurred, and they at once suggested that a place might be made for her in the Ladywell household. They could do with another maid very well, especially as Maud often wanted some assistance with her elaborate toilettes ; and she fancied that Betsy was a handy sort of girl with her fingers, though she had not given her much work of that kind at Thornton House.

Anyone upon whom Mrs. Belassis had trampled, would be sure to be gladly received by Maud ; and under these favourable auspices Betsy Long entered into service at Ladywell Manor.

CHAPTER VIII.

BETROTHED.

A S Tor sat at dinner with Maud and Mrs. Lorraine, about three days after his return from Germany, a pencilled note was brought to him, which he was told had been sent in urgent haste from Mr. Meredith's house.

The note was from Roma, and only contained a few words.

'My father has been taken dangerously ill. He wants you. Can you come at once?

'R. M.'

Tor handed the note to Aunt Olive, and rose from the table.

'I suppose I must go. I hope it may be nothing serious. Poor girl! it is a hard thing for her to be so much alone at a time like this. I will be back as soon as I can. Good-bye.'

Tor strode rapidly along the path which led by a cross-cut to Meredith's house. He did not much like such a summons, for he was always in dread of what the blind man might require of him ; but common humanity forbade him to refuse, when such a message as that had been despatched ; so he walked on, hoping for the best, and trusting that no very awkward questions would arise.

He seemed to be expected at the house, for the servant who admitted him asked no questions, but led him direct to the sick-room.

As he approached it, the door opened, and the doctor came out.

' Ah, Mr. Debenham, I am glad you have come. My patient seems very impatient for your arrival. The sight of you will do him more good than my draught.'

' Is he seriously ill ?'

' Everything is serious with a man whose brain and heart are so abnormally irritable as his. A very slight thing might upset the balance of reason, or do hopeless mischief to the heart. He wants the very closest watching and most perfect quiet both of mind and body. With these, I see no reason why he should not get over this attack ; but if he will work himself up into a fever over any real or imaginary grievance, I will not give *that* for his chance. His daughter seems to understand him thoroughly. I have great confidence in her ; but the morbidly sensitive condition of his mind is a very unfavourable concomitant in his case. I shall look in again before midnight. Do what you can to quiet him. If all goes well during the next six hours, I should say he would do.'

Tor nodded, and went quietly into the room which the doctor had just quitted.

Michael Meredith lay flat upon his back in bed, a strange, ghastly pallor upon his face, and a wandering restlessness in his sightless eyes. His face helped Tor to realize how ill he was, better than the doctor's words had done. He felt shocked and startled at the change he beheld in the familiar countenance.

Roma, as white as a marble statue, stood at the farther side of the bed, bathing her father's forehead with eau de Cologne. The room was pervaded by the odour of strong stimulants and restoratives. The only light was that of a carefully-shaded lamp. Hopelessly blind as Meredith was, he would not permit any glare of light in his room. Even in moments like this, he never lost sight of his love for producing effects.

' Philip Debenham, you have come. It is well !'

This was his greeting, as Tor came and stood beside the bed. The young man took the cold, powerless hand in his strong grasp, and uttered a few kindly and cheering words. There was something reassuring in his strength and vitality, and he possessed that ready gentleness which is the almost invariable attribute of unusual physical power. Father and daughter both felt the better for his presence in the room.

Tor gave his hand to Roma, and looked at her with the grave sympathy of comprehension. Then he crossed over to her, and placed a chair beside the bed.

' Sit down,' he said, with quiet authority. ' You must not waste your strength. Mr.

Meredith, I am going to prescribe for your daughter.'

'Do so—do so!' said Meredith, with gentle satisfaction in his tone. 'She needs more care than I can give.'

Roma certainly looked less white and shaken after she had swallowed the potion Tor mixed for her. The shock and strain that had tried her powers so sorely that day, had begun to make itself felt, and it was time that help should come.

When Tor came round to his old position at the bedside, he fancied that Meredith's face had changed somewhat for the better. Either the extreme ghastliness had passed off a little, or else his eyes had grown used to it.

'You had better sleep if you can, sir,' suggested Tor persuasively. 'I will sit beside you, if that will be any satisfaction. Sleep will restore you better than anything ;' and he drew up a chair and prepared to follow out his own part of the programme.

'Stop!' said Meredith, slowly and softly, as if speaking were still something of an effort ; 'sleep can wait. Sleep will come later. First I must set my mind at rest.'

'Will not you be able to do that better after you have slept?' suggested Tor, who had a distinct dread of what he felt was coming.

'No. I cannot sleep yet. Who knows if I shall ever wake again in this world? I must set my house in order before I go.'

No response was made to this speech by either watcher. Tor fancied that the danger could not be imminent whilst the patient could talk in this strain. He fancied that men who really were dying did not make set speeches to that effect; but Roma's face quivered pitifully, and it needed all her strong self-repression to keep under her emotion. Tor felt a very great compassion for her in her loneliness and devotion. All the chivalry of his nature woke up within him, and urged him to do what he could to lighten the load which lay so heavily upon her.

'Philip Debenham,' said Michael Meredith slowly, 'I withdraw my veto. You have my consent to your wish.'

Naturally, Tor was at a loss to comprehend the drift of this remark. All he could say was :

'I am greatly obliged to you, sir.'

Then came a pause. Meredith seemed to expect the young man to proceed. Tor was trying hard to remember what it was to which the blind man alluded—what veto he could possibly have laid upon any expressed wish of his. He had been quite prepared to hear some allusion to Meredith's wish respecting his marriage with Roma, but not unnaturally he failed to recognise the old subject in its new guise.

'Young hearts should not be severed. I have been selfish in my wish to keep my daughter to myself. Take her now, Philip Debenham. I yield her up to your care. Take her with my blessing, and be a good husband to her, for you have won a pearl amongst women !'

Tor was too much taken aback to make any immediate reply. He glanced at Roma, who sat with hands clasped closely together like one in pain, her head bent, and her face covered with blushes, which were those of misery and humiliation, with nothing in them of maiden shame or joy.

Tor saw at a glance how matters stood

with her—saw that her position was in-
finitely more trying than his ; and his one
desire now was to save her as far as possible
from needless pain.

But Michael Meredith must not be agitated.
Agitation meant death to him at such a time
as the present. Tor was perfectly aware of
this, and had no intention of killing the
father before his daughter's eyes.

Even the short silence which followed his
speech seemed to cause some slight uneasiness
to the sick man.

' You do not speak—you do not answer !'
he said, with a certain sharpness, and a catch
in his breath which showed how easily he was
agitated.

Tor signed to Roma to give him brandy,
and answered gently enough :

' If I do not speak, it is not because I do
not feel. I am deeply conscious of the honour
you do me ; Roma and I both understand all
that your words mean to us. But whilst you
are so ill, we would rather postpone further
discussion. What has passed already is enough
for us.'

The strained look upon the white face

relaxed, and the rapid breathing grew more natural.

'It is well,' he said ; 'dutiful, filial, affectionate! All is very, very well. Roma, give me your hand.'

She obeyed, rising and standing beside the bed, opposite to Tor. Her eyes were lowered, her hand shook a little, yet something in Tor's manner took away the keen edge of her pain and shame.

'Your hand, Philip Debenham,' said Meredith.

Tor placed his own within the sick man's feeble clasp, and thus Michael Meredith had the extreme gratification of joining together the hand of his daughter Roma, and that of the man whom he believed to be Philip Debenham.

'Bless you, my children!' he said fervently.

Roma felt compelled to raise her eyes with imploring deprecation to the young man's face, and found that Tor was smiling down upon her with such a kindly reassurance in his eyes, that she could but smile back, and feel that he at least did not misunderstand her.

Their right hands were still joined. Tor

bent his head over them and kissed—not her hand, but the empty air.

Michael Meredith smiled slowly.

'Have you a ring?' he asked dreamily. 'I should like the pledge to be given and received before my eyes.'

Tor wore Phil's watch and chain, and there was upon it, with Mr. Debenham's seal, a ring which had belonged to his wife. This he disengaged, and placed upon the third finger of Roma's left hand, with another reassuring smile.

Michael Meredith fingered the little antique hoop of chased gold, and his face lighted up with a peculiarly sweet smile.

'Kismet!' he said softly. ''Tis the same ring I sent to Philip Debenham, as a wedding gift to his wife. How all things have come round according to my will! Kiss me, Roma, my child!'

She kissed him silently and passionately; and almost at once he sank into a calm, health-giving sleep; and when Tor had watched him for some considerable time in silence, and saw how much more natural his face had grown, and how tranquilly he breathed, he felt convinced that the worst was over, and that the patient would recover.

For an hour he and Roma had sat silent and motionless on either side of the bed. Tor had been considering how best to put the girl at her ease with him, to show her how completely he understood the situation, and how little need there was for her to trouble herself about the matter. He would arrange everything with the father when he was in a more fit state to hear the truth. She was not to be afraid, for he would make it all right.

This hour of watching gave him ample time to mature his plan, and at the end of it, he wrote a few words upon a slip of paper, and handed it across to Roma.

'I think I had better see you alone for a few minutes before I go. Your father seems much better. Can you leave him for a short time ? I will not detain you long.'

Roma rose at once, after she had read these words, and quietly crossed the room to the door, which opened noiselessly. Tor followed her out, and as soon as she had sent Mr. Meredith's servant into his master's room, she led the way down to the dining-room, where some refreshments had been spread for the watchers.

'Ah, this is well—this is as it should be,' said Tor, looking round with some satisfaction. 'I was summoned away in the midst of my dinner, Miss Meredith, so I am hungry, and you ought to be, whether you are or not. In the character of your affianced husband '—here he smiled in his frankest way—'you must allow me to insist upon your eating something.'

Roma sat down and poured out the tea, which was standing ready. She was confused and unhappy, and Tor was sincerely sorry for her.

'Look here, Roma,' he said, addressing her in a far more brotherly fashion than he ever managed to assume towards Maud. 'I wish you would not make yourself miserable over your father's fancy. I know quite well how it has all arisen, and it is a pity; but, you know, it is no bond, really; only I think, just for the time being, we must humour him by the fiction of an engagement. I hope it is not very distasteful to you. We will keep it as quiet as possible, and I will take the earliest

chance that I can to put matters right. I
know it is hard upon you ; but it seems the
only way.'

'Hard upon me!' echoed Roma ; 'as if that
mattered! I am his daughter; I would do
anything for him—I must ; but you—oh, it
makes me so ashamed!'

'Why should you be ashamed? You
cannot help the curious bent of your father's
mind, nor his feebleness, which makes agitation
so bad for him. We must take things as we
find them, and make the best of his eccen-
tricity. I do not think it is so very bad, after
all. We quite understand one another, and
we can surely be friendly conspirators in our
cause, without being painfully afraid of one
another.'

Roma began to smile in a tremulous sort
of way. 'You are very good to take it like
that. It might have been so dreadful.'

'Dreadful for you, no doubt, though hardly
so for me,' he answered gallantly. Then, to
put her more completely at her ease, he continued gravely, 'No, Roma, you need not be
at all afraid of me ; for I had lost my heart
before ever I saw you, and it is not mine now

to give away. I confide in you, because I am sure that perfect frankness is best between us; but I must ask you to guard my secret jealously, for there are reasons why I cannot make it known as yet to anyone. You see, you are already my chosen confidante, and my only one.'

'Doesn't Maud know?'

'No; and you must not tell her, please.'

'Of course not. I would never say a word to anyone. But—but—suppose she—*she* were to hear something about—about *this*. Would she not—I mean, might it not do harm?'

Tor smiled, as though he were not much afraid.

'I must risk that. No doubt it can be explained all in good time. But there is no need for many people, or any people to know of this little episode. Your father and you have very few visitors; and we shall not be likely to spread the story about. The servants may get an idea and start a rumour; but I think that is all we have to fear; and if you have no objection, I should like to tell Maud the story. I do not keep secrets from her, as a general thing.'

'Oh yes, tell her. I do not mind a bit. I think she ought to know.'

'Thank you, I will let her know how it has happened ; and now that we fully understand one another, and the parts we have to play, is there anything more that I can do for you ?'

Roma passed her hand across her brow, with an action that showed both weariness and bewilderment.

'Thank you, no—I don't think so. You have been very kind, and I am most grateful. But it seems all so strange ; and when I go back to father—and—and if he talks about *this*, what am I to say ?'

'You need say nothing, or hardly anything. Just let him go on his own way, and think his own thoughts. Leave the explanation to me when the right time comes.'

Roma looked at him mournfully.

'You do not know him—you do not know what he is like. The right time will never come. You will never be able to do it without—— Oh, I can't guess what will happen !'

She leaned her forehead upon her clasped

hands, as if to shut out the vision her imagination had conjured up.

Tor looked at her with a compassionate curiosity.

'I wonder, Miss Meredith, if you will think my question a very intrusive one. I cannot help wondering, as I watch you with your father. It seems to me as though you would willingly sacrifice your whole future life, rather than give him one hour's pain. Do you not think that, making every allowance for filial piety, you carry matters rather to an extreme point ?'

'No,' answered Roma, very low. 'For other women it might be so ; but nothing, *nothing* can be too great a sacrifice for me to make for him. I must not shrink from anything.'

'Why is this so ?' asked Tor.

'Because,' and the voice was lower than ever now—'because it is through my fault that he is blind.'

'I should not have asked the question,' answered Tor gently, for he saw that she was much agitated by the tide of recollection which swept over her. 'I beg your pardon. Forget it, and think no more about it.'

'I cannot help thinking—it is never really out of my thoughts when I am with him. I will tell you how it was——'

'Excuse me, Roma, you will do no such thing. I decline to hear the story. We will have no more melancholy reminiscences to-night. Maud will think I am lost if I do not hasten home soon, and I do not mean to go until I have seen you take something to eat and drink. You are as white as a ghost. Your father will think we have had a quarrel already, if you go back to him so limp and spiritless. I am sure he is much better. I quite believe the worst is now past. These heart attacks are very alarming whilst they last, but they are soon over. I will look round in the morning, and see how you are both going on; and if you take my advice, you will not sit up with him. Most likely he will sleep now, and you ought to get a good night's rest too.'

Roma shook her head doubtfully.

'I don't feel as if I could sleep.'

'Why not?'

'Everything is so strange. I can't bear deceiving my father, or seeing you victim-

ized like this ; and I can't see any way out
of it.'

'Miss Meredith, there is no need for you to
see anything at all. All you have to do is
to play your part in the little farce with
which we are humouring him. All the rest
lies with me, and is out of your province
altogether. Leave it to me.'

'I must ; but I dare not think what will
happen.'

'Nothing will happen. Your father will
yield up his desire to make me his son-in-law,
as quietly and willingly as heart could wish.'

Roma shook her head.

'You do not know him, Mr. Debenham, or
you would not say so.'

'It is because I do know him well that I do
say so.'

She made no reply. Tor's manner was so
conclusive, that it seemed useless to dispute
the point.

'You are a very wonderful man,' she said,
after a short pause.

'Sometimes I think so myself,' answered
Tor, with a smile ; 'but I assure you, Miss
Meredith, I am not deceiving you. My reve-

lation to your father, when the time for it arrives, shall not cause him any disappointment or agitation.'

' And when will that moment arrive ?'

' That I cannot tell. It may be soon, or may be late—probably not just yet ; but it depends upon circumstances I cannot now explain. Some day you shall know all, and in the meantime I must ask you to trust me!'

Roma gave him her hand with her rare sweet smile, as she said :

' I should be ungrateful indeed, if I did not.'

Tor looked down at her as he stood holding her hand, and said :

' We shall have to be good friends after this, I think, Roma. Try and feel towards me as if I were your big brother, and I will be a brother to you as far as I know how to play the part. I never had a sister—I mean, practically, until I came back a month or so ago—so that I am new to the part ; but I will play it as well as I can. And you must let me help you with your father, so far as lies in my power, and you must not mind deceiving him a little while for his good.'

'No, I dare not do otherwise; and I should like to feel that you were a sort of brother to me—Philip.'

She spoke the name with a little hesitation, and he smiled approvingly.

'That is right. Now I think we understand one another. I must say good-night; and hope to see you early to-morrow, and to hear a good account of your father.'

So Roma went back to her quiet watch beside the sick man; and Tor strode across the dewy park to tell his story to Maud.

CHAPTER IX.

A GUEST FROM ITALY.

THE next few days passed rather like a dream to Roma. Her father improved slowly but steadily, the tranquil and contented condition of his mind going far towards ensuring his recovery.

Tor came in and out very much as a son of the house might do, and Meredith was entirely satisfied. He did not care to talk or discuss the matter of the sudden betrothal with either daughter or son-in-law elect. He remained passively content, and accepted the fact with the calm superiority characteristic of his habit of mind, and the two most deeply concerned were glad that it should be so.

Roma grew to watch with interest for Tor's visits, and a strong liking sprang up between the two so curiously thrown together. There was not a spark of love (in the ordinary sense of the word) in this friendship. Roma and Tor would never grow sentimental over one another under any circumstances, for the strange, subtle unity of spirit, which is the essence of real love, was entirely wanting between them.

Mr. Meredith had, by his injudicious treatment of the subject, effectually prevented Roma from feeling anything but aversion for the husband he had selected, until Tor's quiet kindness had overcome her repugnance; and he had Maud's image too deeply enshrined within his heart to spare over-much thought or admiration for another woman.

But a very friendly understanding was now arrived at, and Roma was quite willing to accept Tor as a kind of 'big brother,' and to treat him with a frank cordiality that was the surest indication of a mind at ease. The confession which he had made to her, upon the night of their odd betrothal, had been a wise one, for it had taken away all sense of embarrassed discomfort, and given her an interest in him which she could not otherwise have indulged. Altogether, an episode which might have been very painful and trying, had, by a little dexterous management on Tor's part, led to a more comfortable state of mutual understanding than had seemed possible at one time; and Roma gained such confidence in his skill, as well as in his kindliness, that she ceased to trouble her head as to how the matter was to end, feeling certain that he would clear it up all in good time, and in a way which would cause no painful shock to her father's feelings.

Roma was at work again in her studio about a week after her father's sudden illness. Michael Meredith was downstairs again, sleeping quietly in his own small study. The girl had left him, as she could do now, with a mind at ease, and had returned to her work.

She was modelling a bust of Maud Debenham, to give to her brother as a token of friendship and gratitude. Maud had given her a sitting that morning, and she was anxious to get on with the work before the next visit, which was promised for the morrow.

The bust was a great source of delight to the two girls, and its existence was kept a profound secret from the intended recipient.

Roma was hard at work upon the clay, when a servant entered with a card upon a tray.

'It is a foreign gentleman to see master,' was the explanation. 'He cannot speak hardly any English. I think he is Italian by his looks. What shall I do with him? The master is asleep.'

'And he must not be disturbed. I must see the—is he a gentleman, Anne?'

'Yes, ma'am—I think so, by the looks of him; but one can never trust those foreign chaps.'

Roma smiled at this insular prejudice, and looked down at the card. The name was written in the fine characters of foreign penmanship—

Marco Pagliadini.

'I do not think I remember the name; but he may be a friend of father's, from Italy. I must not send him away,' said Roma to herself. Then aloud she added: 'Show the gentleman here, Anne, and let me know when your master is awake.'

A few minutes later, a grave, handsome

young Italian was shown in, who bowed low
to Roma with a stately grace, which had nothing servile in its reverence; and relieved her
at once from the suspicion that the stranger
might be some foreign beggar who had come
to sponge upon her father. This man was
evidently of gentle birth and breeding; and
the girl felt at once at her ease with him.

In her mother's tongue, which was as familiar to her as the English she generally spoke,
she greeted him, with the grave and formal
courtesy which sat more naturally upon her
than the freedom of manner permitted in this
country. Roma had spent most of her life in
Italy, and felt herself more at home with her
mother's countrymen than with her father's.

She bid Signor Pagliadini be seated, and
explained to him that her father had been ill,
and was still very feeble; that he was now
resting, and she feared to disturb him; but
at the same time he must not be deprived of
the pleasure of a visit like the present, and if
the Signor would be so kind as to wait for
half an hour, her father would be delighted to
see him.

The Signor would be delighted to do so, and

expressed himself concerned to hear of the illness of Mr. Meredith. In a short time the two in the studio were talking easily and pleasantly together.

'Did you know my father in Italy?' Roma asked at length. 'I am not sure, but I fancy I have seen your face somewhere.'

'We may possibly have met, Signorina,' answered the Italian. 'For I, too, have been much in Rome; but I had not the honour of personal acquaintance with your father then. I bring with me an introduction from Signor Mattei in Florence. When he heard that I proposed to visit England, he insisted that I should make myself known to the Signor Meredith, who, he tells me, has been settled here for some time.'

'Yes, we have been four years in England,' answered Roma, with a smile and a sigh; 'but I think I like Italy best.'

'I can understand that well,' he answered, looking out into space with his bright, handsome eyes. 'There is no country like our Italy.'

'No, I think not,' assented Roma; and forthwith they fell to discussing its many perfections with a one-sided enthusiasm peculiarly Italian.

Roma meantime studied with a certain artistic pleasure, the handsome head of the young foreigner. He had the thick, dark clustering locks so often seen in Italians, and his hair was rather longer than an Englishman's would be, though not effeminately so. His eyes looked different colours in different lights, but they were good eyes, well formed and expressive, and their long black lashes and thick arched brows added greatly to their force and beauty. His features were good and delicately cut, and the expression of the mouth, so far as it could be seen through the moustache and silky black Vandyke beard, was both frank and sweet. Altogether it was a pleasant face to look upon, and Roma, who was without any 'insular prejudice' where foreigners were concerned, felt that she should like this man, and speculated a little as to who he was, and what could be the object of his visit.

'Are these your works of art, may I ask, Signorina ?' inquired Signor Pagliadini by-and-by.

'Some are mine, and some are my father's,'

answered Roma. 'I have been finishing, as best I can, those that were left incomplete when—when he lost his sight. You know that he has become blind?'

'Signor Mattei told me so much. I was grieved to learn it. It must be a sad affliction to one who loved art so well. I can have a great sympathy for him, for my eyes have suffered from a too close attention to etching, for which work I have a great passion. Even now I cannot use them quite as I would, and a strong light tires them.'

And as he spoke he adjusted his *pince-nez*, the glasses of which were slightly tinged with blue.

'I am sorry,' said Roma.

'But it is nothing—a mere trifle. I am better already, and a little travelling will set me quite to rights. With the Signor Meredith, unfortunately, it is not so.' Then seeing a look of pain on Roma's face, he added quickly, rising at the same time, 'Is this bust the Signorina's work? It is very charming. May I ask if it is the work of imagination, or a portrait?'

'It is an attempt to model a friend of mine,'

Roma answered, smiling. 'I'm afraid it is not very successful. It is not half pretty enough. If you stay any time in this part of the world, Signor, you will be sure to see Miss Debenham of Ladywell Manor. You will then see how much more charming is the original.'

'What name did you say, Signorina?'

'Miss Debenham—Maud Debenham,' answered Roma. 'Perhaps you know her?'

He shook his head.

'No; but I think I know her brother. I knew a Mr. Debenham once—a Mr. Philip Debenham, who was travelling with his friend, a Mr.—Mr.— What was the name?'

'Torwood,' suggested Roma.

'Ah yes—that was the name—Mr. Torwood. I met them in Rome and Naples once. I knew Mr. Debenham well, but his friend not much. That accounts for the likeness—I have been puzzling over that face as I sat here, wondering of whom it reminded me. I see it all now. It is like my friend Filippo. So his sister is a neighbour of yours, is she, Signorina? Then I may hear news of my friend.'

'Yes, Maud is here certainly,' answered

Roma, in a half-puzzled way ; ' but she is not a bit like her brother—not in the very least. Philip Debenham is here too. He came into some property not long since, and has been here about six or eight weeks, I think, taking possession. You will be sure to see him, if you stay ; but he must have changed very much since you knew him, for he is not at all like Maud now.'

Signor Pagliadini smiled with a kind of polite incredulity.

' I do not think a man can change so much as you would represent in a few years ; but then likenesses appeal so differently to different persons. What appears to one a very striking similarity, another will not even see. There, no doubt, lies the whole matter.'

' Perhaps,' answered Roma dubiously ; ' but I cannot think anyone would see any great likeness between Philip and Maud Debenham ; for brother and sister, they are strikingly dissimilar—at least most people think so.'

' Ah, well, I may be wrong ; but I shall be delighted to renew my acquaintance with my good friend. Is Mr. Torwood with him still ? They were constant companions in days of old.'

'Yes ; but they cannot be so now. Mr. Torwood is ill, I believe. I think he is trying German baths or something. Oh yes ; and he has gone on a sea-voyage now. Mr. Debenham went to Germany a little while ago to arrange it. I suppose he will come here for a visit when he is well.'

'My friend Filippo must miss him. He used to follow him about like his shadow.'

'I cannot fancy Philip doing that,' Roma said, with a little laugh. 'He is much too independent. He seems quite happy here, though I am sure he is fond of his friend.'

'I suppose he is too well satisfied with his accession to wealth and importance, to have much thought to spare for anything else.'

'I don't know. I should not think he was that sort of man. I fancy he really liked travelling about better than he likes living in one place. But he knows his duty as a land-owner, and I believe he does it very well. You will find Mr. Debenham very popular here.'

Roma spoke with some little warmth. She fancied, she hardly knew why, that the stranger had thrown some slight disparagement upon Philip Debenham, and she did not approve his tone.

'I think Mr. Debenham always was popular,' assented Signor Pagliadini readily and pleasantly. 'I always found him most interesting and agreeable. I am fond of the English, I think. I am looking forward to my stay amongst them. I wonder if I shall meet any other friends here. I suppose that would be too much good fortune.'

'It is not very likely,' answered Roma. 'For there are very few people at Ladywell—it is quite a remote place. Mr. Belassis has never been abroad, or his family either ; and except for them, there are hardly any more people just round here.'

A few questions about the Belassis family and the neighbourhood kept the ball of conversation going some minutes longer ; but the subject of his friend Philip Debenham was evidently of much greater interest to the stranger, as was but natural, and Roma was telling him a few general facts about the people at Ladywell, when the maid knocked at the door to announce that Mr. Meredith was awake, and would like to see the gentleman.

Roma went to introduce the stranger to her father, and then she retired, leaving the two men to make their own way together.

She had not been long in her studio when a well-known step came ringing down the long passage, and she had barely time to fling a cloth over the bust of Maud, before Tor had entered, as he now did almost at will, greeting her in frank, brotherly fashion.

' Well, Roma, how is the world going with you to-day ?   How is your father ?'

' Better, thanks ;   much more like himself every day.   Have you seen him ?'

' No.   I heard a jabber of Italian going on in his room, so I walked past and came here. Whom has he got with him to-day ?'

' An   Italian   gentleman—an   old   friend   of yours.'

' Of mine ?'

' So   he   says.   He   met   you   in   Italy,   and talks affectionately of his friend Filippo.'

' The devil he does !' breathed Tor to himself ;   but aloud he said, ' Very kind of him, I'm sure.   What's the fellow's name ?'

' Marco Pagliadini.'

' Never heard of him, to my knowledge.'

'You must have a bad memory, for I think you must have known him quite well once.'

'Well, certainly I have known a vast number of foreign fellows at one time or another,' answered Tor, racking his brains in vain to remember the name of Pagliadini in connection with Phil or himself, 'but I certainly have no recollection of this chap.'

'You will remember him when you see him, for he is very good-looking, in an Italian sort of style.'

Tor was not at all anxious to meet this fascinating foreigner, and mentally consigned him to the infernal regions with hearty good-will. If he really had known Phil in past days, he would certainly fail to recognise the present Philip Debenham, and more likely than not would be able again to identify him as Torwood. Altogether, it was as awkward an incident as could well have occurred, this sudden advent of the Italian into the Merediths' household.

'Might have been another Debenham he knew,' suggested Tor, by way of saying something.

'It couldn't be that, because he knew Mr. Torwood too,' answered Roma.

Again Tor registered a mental aspiration that the gentleman and his knowledge might be consigned to a warmer region than that of England, and determined more resolutely than ever to avoid a meeting.

'Well, I dare say I have met him somewhere; but he can't have made a deep impression upon me, as I have no recollection of his name. One doesn't keep all one's acquaintances in one's head for evermore; and as he might be pained by my oblivion, I'd better not meet him, I think. Good-bye, Roma. I'm glad your father is better. I'll come and see him some other day, when I've more time.'

'Must you go now? He will be sorry not to see you. You have hardly been here a minute.'

'Maud wanted me to ride with her as soon as it grew a little cooler. I think I will do so now. That Signor will engross your father quite enough for one day. He ought not to talk too much, you know.'

'Won't you stay and see Signor Pagliadini?'

asked Roma, rather surprised at his decision.

'No, thanks; I don't think I'll bother about it. He'll only detain me longer, and Maud will be disappointed. I will see you again soon. No doubt the Italian converse will cheer your father very much more than my society could do.'

So Tor took his departure in a more precipitate fashion than usual, although his ease of manner did not in any way desert him, and he laughed and chatted with Roma up to the moment of his exit. She rather wondered why he had not stayed to see the Signor; but men were odd, as Maud had always impressed upon her, and did not act as women would do under the same circumstances.

In a short time a summons came for her to join the gentlemen in Mr. Meredith's study. She found that the tea had been carried there; and when she entered, one glance at her father's face showed her how greatly he had been charmed by the stranger's visit.

'Roma, my dear, Signor Pagliadini has kindly consented to become our guest for a few days. He comes, as you know, as an intimate friend of our esteemed relative Alberto Mattei. It is a greater pleasure, Signor, than you can well understand, for a man in my isolated position to receive a visit from one who comes direct from the land of his fondest dreams—from the land where the brightest, the happiest years of his life were spent! Art is my passion—my deepest delight! and the converse with one who knows and loves her well is more to me than you can easily comprehend. Your ready acceptance of the humble hospitality which I can offer, has given me more pleasure than I can well express.'

The stranger made a suitable reply to this flowery address, showing that the advantage was all on his side, and the obligation a very deep one; and after Meredith had made his rejoinder to this declaration, he turned again to his daughter.

' Philip has been here, has he not?'

' Yes, father.'

' I heard his step. I knew he had passed the door twice. How was it he remained so short a time?'

' He was in haste, father. He came to

ask after you, but he was going to ride with Maud.'

'Ah, he is a kind brother. Did you tell him Signor Pagliadini was here?'

'Yes.'

'Signor Pagliadini knows Philip.'

'Yes, so I told him; but he could not wait. However, he will see him another day.'

The Italian smiled in rather an odd fashion.

'My old friend Filippo was not anxious, then, to renew the acquaintance?'

Roma laughed in her quiet way, rather amused at what she thought to be his pique.

'Philip is a thorough Englishman, Signor,' she answered, explaining away, as best she could, what had evidently been taken somewhat amiss. 'He goes his own way in his own fashion, turning neither to right nor left. He had promised to ride with Maud, and ride with Maud he would, in defiance of all other claims upon his time.'

'Ah, just so; I perceive. The sister stands always first. It is quite as it should be.'

'He is very fond of Maud,' said Roma,

thinking he was still offended, trying to lead the conversation into other channels.

'If she at all resembles the statue which you are portraying, it is not to be wondered at, this fraternal devotion.'

'Maud is very charming,' said Mr. Meredith; 'as you will see for yourself some day.'

'And you will find that Philip is just as pleasant in his way, when you do meet him,' continued Roma. 'You must not mind English ways when you come to England, Signor. They are more blunt, perhaps; but I think an Englishman's word is worth its weight in gold!'

The Signor smiled pleasantly.

'My friend Philip Debenham is fortunate in having such a champion.'

Mr. Meredith laughed, and Roma blushed suddenly and vividly.

'We allow our daughters more liberty of speech and action than do your countrymen, Signor. Roma has been brought up *à l'Anglaise*; and then my daughter has the right to defend her friend.'

The Signor bowed and smiled, and Roma blushed still more vividly. She thought it

bad taste on her father's part to give so broad
a hint to a perfect stranger, upon private family
affairs.

Signor Pagliadini seemed to divine her confusion without looking at her, and turned the
conversation into new channels.   He was certainly a fascinating talker.   Roma listened to
him with more pleasure than she had ex-
perienced for many a long day.

The soft language of her childhood was
like music to her ear, and she listened to the
stories of her native land, and the cities in
which her happy early youth had been passed,
with undivided attention.

Michael Meredith dozed in his chair under
the influence of the low musical voice, and
the Italian spoke on, talking only to Roma,
looking into her fair, pale face, and delighting
with all the artistic feeling within him, in
her rare and perfect beauty of form and
feature.

When the blind man awoke to consciousness, more than an hour had passed, and yet
his daughter and their guest were still in
earnest converse.   A stroll round the dewy
garden after dinner, and some music in the

drawing-room later, closed the day ; and Roma went to bed that night feeling as though something very strange had happened to her, and as though some new interest had unaccountably come into her life. This Italian with the soft voice and earnest eyes, that seemed to her half-strange and half-familiar, interested her more than any man whom she had met, since her childhood's dreams had merged into the more definite ideals of woman-hood.

CHAPTER X.

FRIEND OR FOE?

OR left Michael Meredith's house that day with a presentiment that this visit of Signor Pagliadini boded no good to him.

He could not account for the feeling altogether, because by a little dexterous management it would surely be easy to avoid meeting this Italian, who would not be likely to remain more than a single night, or at most two, in so remote a part as Ladywell. Even if he did meet the foreigner, he could but brazen matters out with him as he had done before with Sir Herbert Moncrieff. He would meet the man, if meet him he must, alone, and then there would be no danger that the conversation would be repeated abroad and reach other ears. He knew quite well that if Mrs. Belassis found out that a second old acquaintance had identified him as Torwood, it would enable her to come to a conclusion which was of all things to be avoided. That she already entertained some suspicions about him, her visits to his house in his absence plainly proved. He had been more uneasy than he cared to show, when he heard of her second attempt to be left alone in one of the Ladywell rooms. And the declaration of open enmity, which she had made in a moment of anger, seemed to him to indicate that she knew of something which gave her confidence to declare war. He had ignored in her presence any knowledge of her words or actions ; but for all that he felt ill at ease before her.

Next day news came that Signor Paglia-dini was staying at Mr. Meredith's house, and was an immense favourite there already. Maud had been to see Roma, and had seen him, and been quite captivated by his good looks and gentle manners. Conversation had not flowed easily, as her knowledge of Italian was about on a par with his English ; but Roma had made everything easy, and when the mistress of Ladywell understood that the Signor was an old friend of Phil's, she had asked him up to the Manor House that same afternoon to see her brother.

' I thought you would like me to, Phil,' she said. ' I know your hospitable ways.'

' Quite so—yes ; I shall be glad to see him, though I confess I have no recollection of his name. I may know him when I see him, perhaps.'

' I should think you would be sure to do that. He seemed to know you quite well once.'

Tor was right enough in denying all recollection of the Signor's name. He did not remember to have heard of a Pagliadini in connection with Phil ; but then Phil had a way of picking up foreign friends, about whom Tor never knew much. His easy manners and facile temperament had made Phil very popular everywhere. Acquaintances seemed to crop up round him wherever he went ; and Tor, who, without holding aloof, did not so easily make friends, had often found himself almost a stranger to men who for the moment were quite intimate with Phil.

Pagliadini was probably one of these, and he would not be likely to admit easily that he had been mistaken in the two men. Still, if he was to stay in the neighbourhood, a meeting was inevitable, and it had better take place as early as possible. Ladywell Manor was as good a spot as could be chosen, for a man in his own house feels himself in a better position than he can do elsewhere.

On the whole, Tor considered that Maud had done well to invite the stranger to visit him this same afternoon.

He contrived without any difficulty that Maud and Mrs. Lorraine should be out driving when the Italian appeared; and he received him alone in the small drawing-room, with an ease and friendliness of manner which did him great credit.

Yes, he certainly had known this man somewhere. The first glance showed him so much. He could not recall the circumstances of their former meeting, but there was something undoubtedly familiar in the face, and in the voice too, as soon as the stranger spoke.

Signor Pagliadini entered, and glanced round him in a manner which seemed a trifle disconcerted. Then he smiled, and took Tor's proffered hand.

'I fear I have misunderstood my friends, Signor Torwood. I believed it was my friend Filippo I was to see here. They said you were ill. I am delighted to see you so far recovered. You are no doubt a guest here of the Signor Debenham.'

'On the contrary, Signor, I am the master here—Philip Debenham. Mr. Torwood is certainly ill, I am sorry to say ; but I am not he.'

The Signor received this piece of intelligence with a little smile and shrug.

'The Signor is pleased to joke,' he said. 'Is it that we are masquerading ?'

'No, Signor ; any masquerading that went on was in old days, when my friend Torwood and I used to change names with one another in a foolish, boyish fashion, which now I regret. You may have known my friend under the name of Debenham, but he was really Torwood ; and I am Philip Debenham.'

Tor spoke quietly and firmly ; but he did not like the gleam of distrust that sparkled in

the stranger's eyes. Even the tinted glasses
did not conceal from Tor the glance of
astonishment and disdain which was undoubtedly shot at him. It was evident that
this man might be dangerous, and it behoved
Tor to act towards him with all the firmness
and acuteness which lay in his power.

'You are perplexed, I see, Signor, by my
statement,' he said courteously.

'I am, Signor.'

'But why so, may I ask? Is it not enough
when I tell you that I and my friend were
more than once foolish and thoughtless enough
to change our names one for the other?
The whole matter lies there, if you can but
see it.'

Signor Pagliadini made a little deprecating
foreign bow, as if to apologize for any doubt
he might cast upon his host's veracity; but
all his grace of manner could not hide from
Tor the distinctly menacing look in those half-
concealed eyes of his.

'I could see that well enough, Signor,' he
said, with a certain unpleasant significance in
manner. 'It certainly seems an odd sort of
amusement for grown men, this interchange of

names.   It does not sound very amusing, or
profitable either.   Still, of course, if the
Signor says it was so, why then, without
doubt, so it was.   But still, I may be stupid
—I do not see things quickly—I make hillocks
into mountains, very likely, as you English
say; but I cannot understand one thing.'

'And what may that one thing be?'

'I cannot understand how it comes about
that your charming sister and my old friend
Filippo—who is, I hear, Mr. Torwood—are so
strikingly alike.   Even for brother and sister
—which you say they are not—such a likeness
would be remarkable.'

The Italian was staring hard at him, but
Tor was on his guard, and his face betrayed
nothing.   He merely smiled a little.

'Are you not rather imaginative, Signor?'

'Not that I am aware of.'

'Well, I don't know.   It seems so to me.
I have not observed any striking likeness.'

Signor Pagliadini smiled a pleasant smile.

'No, Signor; it is quite to be expected that
you have not.'

'What do you mean, sir?'

Tor liked neither the words nor the tone.

' I mean that near relatives seldom see likenesses,' he answered, with a reassuring smile.
' It is strangers who do that, not intimates.'

Tor was silent, thinking out his plan of
action. He was perfectly aware that he was
suspected; he already felt in a great measure
at this man's mercy, and he believed him to
be, for some unknown reason, his enemy.
He dared not make a confidant of a perfect
stranger, who might be anything, from a spy of
Belassis, upwards; and yet he must endeavour
to keep on friendly terms, and if it were possible bind him over to silence. If he were to
talk abroad as he was talking here, a catas-
trophe would be inevitable.

' Sit down, Signor,' he said courteously. ' I
see I must have some further talk with you.
Let us be frank with one another. Do not be
afraid to speak out. Truth is always the
best. You believe that I am an impostor—is
it not so?'

' That is your word, not mine, Signor,' said
the Italian. ' You know best if the cap fits—
as your proverb goes.'

' If it is my word,' returned Tor quickly,
' it but expresses your own thoughts, unless I

have very much misread your face and your words.'

'What can I think, in the face of these facts?' asked the stranger, with the significance of voice and look which Tor greatly disliked. 'The Signor puts me in a very awkward position by asking such questions.'

Tor laughed, in spite of his inward discomfiture.

'Pardon me, Signor; I think it is you who put me in an awkward position by your insinuations. I am sure you cannot mean to insult me; but if you will think the matter quietly over, you will see, I think, that what you would imply about me, is about as great an insult as one man can offer to another. You seem to me to suggest that I am playing an impostor's part, living in my friend's house, trading upon his fortune, adopting his name. Come, come, Signor Pagliadini, when one comes to put it all into plain words, I think you must see for yourself how utterly absurd and unfounded such an idea must be. Why, the thing would be impossible!'

'It has been done before now, I believe,' answered the stranger.

Tor drew himself up haughtily.

'Do you mean to say that you accuse me of doing so great a wrong as this to my best friend?'

The stranger rose too, and faced Tor with sparkling eyes.

'Will you give me your word of honour that you are not doing him a great wrong?'

'I will,' answered Tor firmly; and he held his head proudly, as one who knows that he speaks the truth. 'I give you my word of honour, as an Englishman and as a gentleman, that I have never wronged my friend even in thought. I would cut off my right hand sooner than commit a single act dishonourable to our old friendship!'

The Italian's face softened somewhat, and he sat down again with what sounded like a sigh.

'Signor,' he said, with a slight bow, 'I accept your word. I must accept such an asseveration as that. I have been taught to believe in an Englishman's word, and I will try to do so.'

'I am obliged by your concession, Signor. It is not a pleasant thing to be doubted or suspected, however innocent one may be in reality. And now that you have done me the honour to believe me, I will point out to you how impossible your theory of imposture must be. If things were as you would have implied, why should Philip Debenham permit such a substitution of names and places ? If I were an impostor, surely the true man would come forward and claim his own.'

Signor Pagliadini shot a quick look at him, and said :

' Undoubtedly so—*if he could.*'

' What do you mean, Signor ?'

' I understood your friend was ill.'

' Yes ; so he is.'

' Perhaps that might account for his passive condition.'

Tor smiled, and shook his head.

' Hardly likely, if you come to consider it.'

' We are not going to re-open the argument, Signor,' said the Italian quietly. ' I have told you I am satisfied by the pledge you have given me. Appearances are undoubtedly against . you, but we all know that appearances are deceptive. Unless circumstances force me to a different conclusion, I shall accept the one I have already arrived at.'

'And in return, may I ask a personal favour from you?'

'Certainly.'

'May I ask you not to discuss with other people the circumstances which you deem so strange? I think you can see for yourself that to raise a doubt as to my identity would be at the present moment very unpleasant for me?'

'Very,' assented the Italian drily.

Tor felt disposed to give way to a natural desire to knock the fellow down; but he controlled himself, and continued quietly:

'When Mr. Torwood returns from the voyage on which he has started for his health, the whole world is welcome to say what it likes. When he is here to answer for his identity, as I can answer for mine, I do not care one iota for what anybody may please to say. He and I can convince everyone who wishes convincing, as to who and what we are. But whilst he is away, and beyond the reach even of letters, I would much rather nothing was said which could raise such a doubt in my friend's mind. Not that I care so very much about it;' and here Tor held his head up proudly. 'I can hold my own, I flatter myself, before the world, and in defiance of any doubts anybody likes to cast upon me. You are welcome to say and do what you choose. I am not going to sue to any man; but I advise you, for your own sake, to take care what you do, because I am better as a friend than as an enemy; and I am honest enough to tell you candidly, that to raise a doubt as to my right to my name would be unpleasant for me during Torwood's absence, and that if you raise that doubt, you will gain a tolerably dangerous enemy.

The Italian was silent awhile. He was, perhaps, surprised at this sudden outburst. Tor believed this declaration of strength and independence had done good to his cause, for Signor Pagliadini looked at him with more of respect and less of mockery than he had done before.

'Signor Debenham,' he said gravely, 'it is not my wish to cause you any needless annoyance. I may be puzzled—I may not trust you altogether as a friend—but I have no

wish to be your enemy. I will not be
treacherous. I will not take you by surprise. If I have anything to announce to
the world, I will announce it to you first in
private.'

Tor smiled, and bent his head in seemingly
somewhat ironical gratitude. In reality, he
was really grateful for this pledge.

He could carry things off with a high hand
to a certain point ; but beyond that he dared
not go. He knew if any enemy of his once
got hold of the idea that this man evidently
possessed (that he was merely masquerading as
Philip Debenham, being in reality Torrington
Torwood)—if Mrs. Belassis, or any enemy of
his, had this idea once put into their minds,
then in truth it would be hard to brazen
out his part. Close cross-examination must
bring out the truth. Beyond a certain point no
cleverness nor coolness could carry him; and
it was something to gain the promise Pagliadini had voluntarily made. If the worst came
to the worst—if the Italian did discover his
secret, he could but tell him the whole truth,
and throw himself upon his mercy. If he
were really Phil's friend, he would most likely

be ready to become an ally. If not Phil's friend, what interest could he possibly have in the matter ?

These thoughts flashed through Tor's mind in a few seconds. He was not, however, going to show any open gratitude for the admission just granted. All he said was :

' I agree with you entirely, Signor. Whatever passes upon this subject had better be discussed privately between us two, before being given to the world at large. And now that this rather awkward conversation is at an end, and we have come to a satisfactory conclusion, will you allow me the pleasure of showing you round the garden? There is a good deal worth looking at there.'

The interruption was welcome to both men. It was not pleasant, after what had just passed, to sit there facing one another, trying to keep up a conversation on indifferent subjects.

Whilst walking leisurely upon the terraces and in the shady shrubbery paths, it was easier to establish easy relations ; and the Italian showed a great deal of intelligent interest in all he saw.

He admired the whole place very heartily;

seemed struck by the knowledge Tor had so quickly acquired, and was altogether both friendly and pleasant.

Tor was more and more convinced that he had known this guest of his before, although he failed to recall the name. Voice, manner, and expression all seemed in a manner familiar, and left an impression upon his mind that he had liked as well as known the Signor at some distant date.

When the ladies returned, the men joined them at their tea, and Maud seemed much struck by the handsome Italian, and made so much of him that Tor was half inclined to feel jealous. Although he could not speak it, Signor Pagliadini understood English very fairly, and seemed pleased and flattered by the way in which she chattered away to him.

When he had gone, she had a great deal to say about his handsome eyes, and soft voice, and courtly manners. Tor was somewhat silent and absent; but she did not seem to observe it, and was rather startled by the sudden way in which he changed the subject.

'Maud,' he said, 'do you think you and
Aunt Olive would mind very much if I were
to bring some lady-visitors to Ladywell ?'

'Lady-visitors !' echoed Maud. 'Why,
Phil, what an odd suggestion from a confirmed
old bachelor like you ! Of course we shall
be delighted—we always are delighted to do
your bidding. But who are they ? and why
do you want them ?'

'They are Miss Marjory Descartes and her
niece, whose name I forget; but I think I must
include her. I like Miss Marjory immensely,
as you know; and I feel inclined to ask her to
come and spend a week here, before she has
time to forget the favourable impression I
produced upon her in Whitbury.'

'Yes, dear boy, have her by all means. I
wish you joy,' answered Maud sweetly and
slily. 'But, Phil dear, don't you think she's
just a little bit *old* for you ?'

'Well, I must consider the point,' answered
Tor, with a smile. 'She is wonderfully
young for her years, and I'm not at all sure
that she couldn't outwalk you, even now,
Maud, and I know she could beat you at
tennis. However, we will make up our minds

on that subject later ; and in the meantime you don't mind my asking her here ?'

'As if I ever minded anything you did, Phil !' laughed Maud. 'I shouldn't mind if you turned the whole house into a menagerie, and brought up young lions in the drawing-room, if only you'd stay yourself and keep us in order. Everything is so flat and stale when you go away. I can't think how auntie and I ever lived without you !'

'Well,' returned Tor, with a smile that showed genuine satisfaction, 'if you don't mind who I am, or what I do, so long as I remain upon the spot, I have not much to ear.'

'To fear indeed!' laughed Maud, laying her little hands caressingly upon his two shoulders, and looking up at him with smiling eyes. 'I don't believe you know what fear is, Phil. I don't believe you could be afraid of anything or anybody, you great, big, strong boy. You are like the everlasting Bayard one gets so tired of hearing about—*sans peur et sans reproche*—only you really are so ; and half the people one hears it said of are nothing of the kind.'

He bent his head and kissed her on the forehead, and then strolled off by himself to think matters over.

His idea of asking Miss Marjory down, was a sudden inspiration on his part. He had felt that the present threatened crisis required very careful watching on his part, and that two heads were better than one. He had a great opinion of Miss Marjory's shrewdness, and was confident that she would be a zealous partizan in any cause she had once taken up.

Circumstances prevented him from taking anyone else into his confidence. Much as he would be relieved by discussing the position with Maud or Mrs. Lorraine, he felt that he must not be weak enough to gratify the wish.

The fear and anxiety which it would occasion them, and the embarrassment his assumed relationship must cause, would be, he felt, too great a burden to ask them to bear, and they ought not to be put in so trying a position. Then every additional person let into the secret meant additional chances of its innocent betrayal ; and more danger was certainly to be avoided, not courted.

Miss Marjory, however, did know all, and had promised her assistance if ever it should be required; and Tor felt as though that moment had now come.

So he wrote his letter, explaining what had occurred, asking Miss Marjory's opinion as to the motive the stranger could have had in accusing him of the imposture, and speculating whether it was by accident or by design that he had found his way to Ladywell.

He concluded his letter thus :

' I do not like to remind you of your promise to come and help me if danger threatened, beeause I do not yet know if there is any real danger to be apprehended. At the same time I promised to let you know if anything un-foreseen occurred to disturb me, and that promise I now fulfil.

' If you will accept an invitation to Lady-well for any time you think good to fix, I shall be more deeply in your debt than even at present ; but I must not trespass too far upon your kindness, and plead my personal woes more than circumstances warrant. I will only add that a visit from you and your niece would be more of a pleasure and relief at this juncture than I can well express.

         'Yours very sincerely,

            'PHILIP DEBENHAM.'

When that letter was written, Tor's spirits rose. He had great confidence in Miss Marjory, and he believed she would come.

CHAPTER XI.

MRS. BELASSIS FINDS AN ALLY.

TWO days later Mrs. Belassis, and Betsy Long held a secret meeting under an oak-tree in a secluded corner of the park.

'Well, Betsy,' said the ex-mistress graciously, 'have you anything to tell me yet?'

'Well, ma'am, I don't know as it's anything you'll care to hear ; but I can't help thinking there's something odd about the foreign gentleman as is staying down at Mr. Meredith's.'

'A foreign gentleman?' repeated Mrs. Belassis. 'I have not heard of him. Who is he?'

'I suppose he's a friend of Mr. Meredith's. Folks say so. Anyway, he is staying down

there.   But I believe he's come to see master,
really.'

'Why ?'

'Well, he came to see him two days ago.
He was took into the little drawing-room, and
I was in the big one, doing a bit of dusting
I'd forgotten in the morning ; for I knew
Miss Debenham and Mrs. Lorraine had gone
out driving.'

'Could you hear what passed ?'

'I could hear a good deal; but I couldn't
understand a word, for 'twas all in some
foreign language—Italian, I suppose; but I'm
quite sure those two gentlemen weren't
strangers to one another, or they'd never have
gone on as they did.'

'How did they go on?'

'Well, they talked and talked, and seemed
to get quite excited-like, and once I thought
they were going to quarrel, and I peeped
through the curtains.   There they were, standing glaring at one another like two wild
beasts; and Mr. Debenham, he had his head
back in that masterful way of his, and was
speaking as proud as proud could be.   I
thought the foreign gentleman was a bit scared

by the look in his eyes, for he seemed to knock under then; but they went on talking for ever so long.'

' Do you think they did quarrel ?'

' If they did, they must have made it up afterwards, for by-and-by they went round the garden together, and had tea with the ladies when they got back. But James, he said as master looked very grave all dinner-time, and hardly talked at all.'

Mrs. Belassis pondered over this communication; but Betsy had not come to the end of her revelations, and did not give her mistress much time for thought.

' There's something about that foreign gentleman as master doesn't like, *I* know,' continued the girl; ' for he hadn't long gone before master shut himself up in his study to write letters. He was there up till the dressing-bell rang; and just as I was going in for the letters, which is part of my work—I collects them from the ladies and from master, and puts them in the box ready for the man—I met him coming out of his room. " There's only one letter, Betsy," he said; and so there was, and he'd only just finished it, for the ink

wasn't hardly dry; and it was addressed to
" Miss Marjory Descartes," at a place beginning
with W.   I can't remember the name.'

'Whitbury?' suggested Mrs. Belassis, looking aroused and almost excited. 'Go on,
Betsy; I see you have more to tell.   You have
been very clever, and I shall not forget it.'

Betsy curtseyed, and drew a few steps
nearer, as she made her next communication
in a lowered voice.

'I turned the letter over; and it had been
done up so quickly that the gum hadn't
hardly stuck.   I gave a little pull, and it
came open in my hands.'

A look of intense interest came over Mrs.
Belassis' face.

'And you read the letter?   What did it
say?'

'Well, ma'am, I'm no particular scholar,
and the letter was too long for me to read
through.   I was in a mortal fear as somebody would come and catch me.   If it hadn't
been dressing-time, I'd not have dared to do
so much as I did.'

'Well, go on, Betsy.   What did you make
out?'

' The master, he wrote all about the foreign gentleman, and I'm main sure he didn't like his coming, not a bit. He talked about danger, and not understanding what was coming, and ended up by asking the lady to come and see him. I couldn't make out no more than that; but I'm quite sure as it was all about the strange gentleman, and that master had been regular put about by his coming.'

' Ah !' said Mrs. Belassis, and said no more, because her thoughts were too confused as yet to admit of the interpretation of words.

Betsy, who saw that she had made an impression, proceeded to deepen it. She was enjoying very much her own cleverness, and the sense of importance that her position gave to her.

' I fastened up the letter pretty quick again, and put it in the box; but I couldn't get the thing out of my head. In the evening I took a walk in the park, as I often do, and there's one of the gardeners as has sometimes come and had a talk with me. He's a nice respectable young man, and I don't mind having a little chat with him now and again.

Well, ma'am, that evening, as I was waiting about amongst the trees, watching the shadows get longer and darker, I thought I saw the young man a-coming, and I went to meet him; but when I got close up, why, I saw it was somebody all muffled up with a great silk handkerchief, and he seemed sneaking up towards the house, as if he didn't want to be seen. I was behind him, and I came so soft that he didn't hear me, and passed by; but I knew quite well who he was. It was the gentleman who had been with master in the afternoon, and it's my opinion he hung for hours about the house before he went; and I'm almost sure I saw him in the shrubbery last night, too!'

A little cross-examination convinced Mrs. Belassis that Betsy was speaking the truth, and she left the girl in a very contemplative frame of mind, after bidding her keep a sharp look-out, and notice particularly how often the stranger visited Ladywell, and how many private interviews he held with Mr. Debenham.

' There is something odd about this,' said Mrs. Belassis to herself. ' That foreigner knows something which Philip wishes hushed up. That is evident, I think. The point is, what on earth can Miss Marjory Descartes have to do with it ? If she visits Ladywell, perhaps I can find that out for myself; meantime I must leave that question. But I will see this foreigner. I will call on Michael Meredith and inquire after him, as he has been so ill. I do not frequently visit the house; but I do not see, under the present circumstances, that my doing so can attract any suspicion.'

Mrs. Belassis walked on thoughtfully for awhile, and then added, with an air of determination :

' Yes, I will go now, morning though it be. All times are alike to the blind. Perhaps a little dexterous flattery will induce Meredith to ask me to luncheon, and then I shall see this strange guest. I much want some conversation with him. I wish I could speak Italian ; however, no doubt French will suit my purpose just as well.'

When Mrs. Belassis had planned a certain course of action, it was not often that she failed to carry it through.

The Merediths and the Belassis' were not

on intimate terms, but there had never been
any coldness between them. Michael Meredith
did not trouble himself with matters which
did not concern him; and Maud's complaints
about her uncle and aunt never made any
impression upon him, neither did he pay any
heed to the hints he heard dropped from time
to time as to the honesty of the ex-lawyer.
His own finances were not in the hands of
Belassis. He had never heard that his old
friend Debenham had doubted his brother-in-
law's integrity; and so he had no grudge
against Belassis, and always received his wife
or daughters with his customary gentle *em-
pressement.*

Mrs. Belassis could be very suave and
gentle when it suited her purpose; and her
concern over the blind man's illness, her
anxiety to learn its every detail, and the
interest she evinced in the whole subject, quite
won Meredith's heart; for if there was one
thing he loved to discuss more than another,
it was himself and his sensations, and a
new and interested listener was an immense
acquisition.

Mrs. Belassis skilfully led him on to speak

more and more, until the luncheon-bell broke in upon the interview, and with an apology for her lengthy visit she rose to depart.

' No, no, my dear madam ; indeed I cannot permit you to leave so suddenly. Your kind visit has quite cheered me up. You really must remain and partake of our simple midday meal. I want to introduce to you my young friend Signor Pagliadini, who is at present our guest. He is a most intelligent young man, quite an acquisition to the neighbourhood ; only, unluckily, he does not speak English.'

' Who is he ?' asked Mrs. Belassis, with interest.

' A young Italian, of good birth and considerable wealth, I believe. A relative of my wife's, Signor Mattei of Florence, knows him, and sent him to me with an introduction. He has known him for many years, and speaks highly of his talent and love of art.'

' Is he going to make any stay here ?'

' I do not think his plans are made ; but I hope to induce him to be my guest for some days to come. Philip, I think, will join with me in persuading him to remain in our part of

the world; for he knows him well, I find.   They
were quite intimate friends, I believe, at one
time.'

'Indeed!'

'Yes; he speaks very highly of our dear
Philip, as everyone does.   I think my dear
Roma is to be congratulated, as well as Philip,
upon the way in which matters have turned
out.'

'What!'

'Ah, did you not know ?   Well, young
people do like a little bit of mystery and secrecy,
so I must not betray them.   However, my dear
madam, we have not grown so old, you and I,
that we have lost our sympathy for the first
romance of a young love.   And now, let me
give you my arm to the dining-room, and I
shall then have the pleasure of making known
to you my young Italian friend.'

When Mr. Meredith and his companion
made their quiet entrance into the next room,
Mrs. Belassis caught one glimpse of two dark
heads bent very closely together over a lovely
bunch of roses and heliotrope, which was being
transferred from his hands to hers.   The blind
man was no hindrance to any such small pass-

ages as these ; but Roma's cheeks flamed
crimson when she saw that her father was not
alone, and the ardent look in the young
Italian's eyes was not lost upon Mrs. Belassis.

The introduction passed off easily, and the
conversation was carried on in French, so as to
be intelligible to Mrs. Belassis.

' What lovely flowers, Miss Meredith !' said
their guest, not altogether without malice.
' Are they from your garden ?'

' I had the honour of presenting them to
Mademoiselle,' answered the Italian gravely.
' They came from the garden of my esteemed
friend, M. Debenham.'

' Oh, have you been to see Philip again ?'
asked Meredith. ' You go there very often.
You must find a great deal to say to one
another.'

' I have not seen my friend to-day,' answered
the Signor ; ' but I took the liberty of helping
myself to his flowers without leave.'

' You have courage, Monsieur,' remarked
Mrs. Belassis, with rather a keen look.

' That is a virtue much esteemed in your
country—is it not so, Madame ?' he asked.
' Or have I taken an unpardonable liberty ?'

' That is for my nephew to decide, not for
me.   No doubt you know best how far your
friendship warrants such an act.'

' Madame is right,' answered he, meeting her
searching gaze with one equally keen and significant.   ' I think I know how far I may go
with my friend Filippo.'

She could not be certain of it, but she had
an idea that more was meant than met the ear.
Her suspicion that this man knew more of
Philip's private history than appeared, was
gradually strengthened by what followed.

' You know my nephew well—is it not so?'

' I once knew Philip Debenham well, inti-
mately I might say ; but the master of that
great house yonder—I cannot say he is a great
friend of mine.'

' How do you mean, Monsieur ?'

The Italian smiled and shrugged, with a
gesture far more significant than words.

' Ah, Madame, we all learn the lesson of
life ; times change, and friends too—with circumstances such as these, it is often the case.'

' Has Philip Debenham changed so much ?'

' So it appears to me ; but I may be mistaken.   My memory may be defective.'

' I do not think Philip could ever have been so very different from what he is now,' said Roma. ' He strikes me as a man who would change singularly little. He is so independent of other people and their opinions.'

' Mademoiselle is perfectly right there,' answered the Italian. ' He goes his own way, without in any way considering what may be the effect upon others.'

Roma smiled and shook her head. Her colour was a little warmer than usual. She was perfectly aware that the Signor was jealous of Philip Debenham. There was no need that he should be so ; but she could not tell him that, and she could not be very hard upon him if he did feel somewhat bitter against his rival. Roma knew well that this man loved her, and his love gave her a deep-seated sense of joy, as well as some embarrassment and pain.

Mrs. Belassis, however, put quite a different interpretation upon his words.

' Was it always so with him ?' she asked.

' On the contrary, he was once the kindest and best of friends. This is quite a new development.'

'The pride of his new position, perhaps.'

'Yes ; a position such as his must have its grave difficulties. My friend is very bold, but I am not sure whether he has not undertaken more than he can grapple with.'

'I am quite of that opinion myself,' said Mrs. Belassis, still trying to read the face before her, whilst she grew more and more convinced that the stranger held the clue to the mystery whose existence she had only vaguely guessed. From the readiness he evinced to talk on the subject, Mrs. Belassis argued that he was looking out for an ally to assist him in some attack upon the false friend, and only too ready was she to support him in such an attempt.

She must contrive to secure a private interview—that must be the first step ; and fortune certainly favoured her this day, for when she rose to take her departure, Signor Pagliadini rose likewise, and begged for the honour of escorting her to her own house.

Side by side the two newly-made acquaintances passed out of sight of the house, silent at first, because a sudden sense of restraint seemed to have fallen upon them ; but even this silence encouraged Mrs. Belassis in her theory, and she determined to make a bold plunge and see the effect.

'Monsieur,' she began slowly and significantly, 'I am quite ready to help you.'

'Madame is good to say so ; but I do not quite comprehend.'

'I think that you do, Monsieur.'

They paused by mutual consent, and looked at one another keenly and steadfastly.

'Will Madame sit down¦?' asked the Italian, indicating a fallen tree-trunk which lay beside the hedge. The narrow lane was shady and secluded, and it was not likely that anyone would pass by to disturb them. 'We had better understand one another. May I ask in what way Madame proposes to assist me ?'

'Your object, Monsieur, if I mistake you not, is to repair some great injustice which my nephew has committed against his friend. Am I not right so far as I go ?'

'I will not say that Madame is altogether deceived ; but I should like to know on what grounds you suspect your nephew.'

Mrs. Belassis hardly knew how to put into words her vague suspicions. She would much rather that her companion suggested the nature of the injustice. She tried to draw him out.

'I have been frank with you, Monsieur, and have told you that I suspect my nephew. Is not that enough? It is your turn now to tell me what it is you have discovered, that will bear upon our suspicion.'

But the bait did not take.

'Our suspicion is doubtless the same. I am aware that one does not like to put it into words. May I ask further against which of Mr. Debenham's friends Madame believes this injustice to have been done?'

'Against Mr. Torwood, of course.'

The sudden flash of some emotion, which she could not fathom, passed over the stranger's face as she uttered the name, and convinced Mrs. Belassis that she had been right in her surmise.

'Quite so, Madame. It is his old friend Mr. Torwood whom he has injured—the friend to whom he owes so much. Your suspicion is correct.'

'Did you know Mr. Torwood once?'

'Slightly—yes.'

'Do you know where he is now?'

'I do.'

A look of triumph gleamed in Mrs. Belassis' eye.

'Good,' she said, with an air of satisfaction. 'Philip Debenham asserts that he is on board some sailing-vessel upon a sea-voyage. I do not believe he is in any such place. I am convinced that the sea-voyage is simply a blind.'

'Madame is again right—perfectly right. Mr. Torwood is not at sea at present. The sea-voyage exists only in the vivid imagination of his friend.'

'Ah!' Mrs. Belassis drew a long breath. 'Monsieur,' she said eagerly, 'tell me, where is Mr. Torwood?'

'Madame, you shall know that also in due time. At present, I may not reveal his abode.'

Mrs. Belassis hardly felt this check, in her excitement and triumph.

'You know where he is, Monsieur? You could lay your hand upon him at any moment?'

'At any moment, Madame. When the

time comes the man shall come forward. Philip Debenham and Torrington Torwood shall stand face to face.'

'May I be there to see !' breathed Mrs. Belassis ; and after a brief pause she added : 'Is Mr. Torwood in England, then ?'

'He is.'

'He has escaped from the restraints put upon him by *his friend ?*'

A curious flash passed over the young man's face, as he answered steadily :

'He has.'

Mrs. Belassis would like to have known more, but it was now the stranger's turn to ask questions.

'Madame,' he began, and the tone, although quite respectful, had in it a certain ring of authority, which obliged Mrs. Belassis to be more candid than perhaps she had at first intended, 'if we are to work together, we must understand one another. I have a motive in what I do. A friend of mine has been wronged, and I am anxious to assist him to his rights again ; my motive for what I do is friendship. But you do not know Mr. Torwood. Philip

Debenham is your nephew and near neighbour—why is it you are so anxious to disgrace
him ?'

Mrs. Belassis was somewhat taken aback by
this home-thrust ; but she was equal to the
occasion.

' I will tell you, Monsieur.   As you say, we
must be frank with one another; and I will
not pretend that an abstract love of justice
alone actuates me, for it would not be true, and
you would not believe me.   No; I have a
grievance against Philip Debenham, and it is
this.   He has been more ungrateful to me
and to my husband than you would believe
possible.   He owes us almost everything, for
from the age of ten years, he was adopted by
us, and brought up like our own child.   He was
educated abroad by his own wish ; and after
eight years of school and college life, we found
him an excellent berth in a merchant's office.
This not being grand enough for my lord, who
had not a penny of his own, he ran away and
lived for eight years upon the charity of Mr.
Torwood, whom he is now using so badly.   Then
he succeeded to a large fortune and property,

and came back to this place, and has behaved with studied ingratitude to us ever since, openly accusing his uncle of frauds, which no doubt he would have perpetrated himself in the same situation. I need not say that we feel such base ingratitude keenly, and that for my husband's sake I am justly indignant. When I find that he is spending Mr. Torwood's money almost more freely than his own, I confess I do wish to see him brought to book.'

A step came tramping down the lane, and Tor's tall figure emerged suddenly into view. He gave one quick glance at the two persons seated upon the fallen tree, lifted his hat and passed by without a word.

'A handsome man!' said Mrs. Belassis, looking after him with an evil light in her eyes. 'One would not think, to look at him, what a load of guilt he was carrying about with him.'

Tor's appearance seemed quite to have broken up the conference. Signor Pagliadini, with a preoccupied air, made his adieu, and left Mrs. Belassis to finish her walk alone.

'Spends Torwood's money almost more freely than his own,' slowly repeated the Signor, in Mrs. Belassis' French phrasing; and then he added, in good vigorous English, 'The deuce he does!'

CHAPTER XII.

MISS MARJORY'S OPINIONS.

'AND now,' said Miss Marjory briskly, 'let me hear what has happened, or is going to happen, that makes you so anxious.'

Miss Marjory and her niece had arrived at the Manor House a few hours before; but Tor had not been able, until now, to secure her undivided attention. Maud and Mrs. Lorraine had been so much amused by her conversation, that it had been impossible to secure any privacy, and it was only when Miss Marjory's enthusiasm over the garden and the hot-houses had tired out the less comprehending and interested part of the company, that Tor found himself alone with his guest.

'It is so good of you to come so quickly,' said he, with real gratitude in his tone. 'I feel as though I really did need an ally at the present threatened crisis. I cannot thank you enough.'

' Oh, I shall make it worth my while to have come. I shall leave you laden with spoil, I can see. There are ever so many things I have seen already that I want, and haven't got. I shall take cuttings innumerable, with or without your leave. Your orchids make me break the tenth commandment on the spot. I think I must put up an orchid-house myself. Oh yes, I will make a good thing of this visit —never fear !'

' If you will let me put up an orchid-house for you, as a slight——'

' Stuff and nonsense! I'm not going to let you do anything ridiculous and romantic. Too much glass might be more of a hindrance than a help to the letting of the house in the future. Now look here—we are alone at last : tell me what is the matter, and what it is I can do for you.'

' The matter is, that a foreign chap has turned up here—a Signor Pagliadini ; he says he knew Phil and me abroad, and I believe that's true enough, for I know his face, though

I can't recollect him exactly. But he knows, too—of that I am convinced—who I really am, and will not swallow the fiction I try to force upon him. In addition to this, I believe he has a spite against, me and comes with a motive ; and though he doesn't speak out, I am pretty certain that he knows a great deal more than he has any business to, and that he means mischief.'

' Why?'

' By the ugly hints he gives, and by his significant looks and words. And then I came upon him and Mrs. Belassis in deep talk by the roadside; and by the startled look she cast at me, I know of whom it was they were talking.'

' We can soon stop the Belassis' mouths,' remarked Miss Marjory grimly. ' I think we can give them ample food for meditation on their own account.'

' Have you found anything out about the first wife?'

' I have found out that in February, 1850, she was alive and fairly well. I am making inquiries, and I think I soon shall be able to ascertain the date of her death ; but it strikes

me that your virtuous uncle has run it very
fine. I should not wonder if he finds himself
in a desperately nasty position.'

'Something like what I find myself in now,'
said Tor, shaking his head.

'Now, don't you get low about it,' advised
Miss Marjory, with the air of a benig-
nant Minerva. 'You'll never do anything
if you lose heart. For my part, I rise to the
occasion. I know I have a natural talent for
intrigue, though circumstances have not
hitherto been favourable to its development.'

'I am glad you have,' smiled Tor, 'for my
powers seem deserting me. That confounded
Italian—I beg your pardon, but I feel strongly
upon the subject—with his smooth tongue and
offensive hints, bothers me tremendously. I
know he is my enemy, and will injure me if
he can.'

'Have you ever made an enemy that you
know of?' asked Miss Marjory.

Tor reflected a little.

'I shouldn't say exactly that,' he answered.
'I have had occasional disputes with different
men at different times. When my blood is
up, I speak my mind pretty freely, and lay it

on thick; but then, I don't think I am easily
roused to wrath, and I have no recollection of
any row likely to have made an eternal enmity
between me and another fellow. No, I have
no clue at all to his motive, but I am quite
certain he has one, and possesses some knowledge of the truth; he would not go on as he
does, if he was actuated merely by a curiosity
to know why I was called "Torwood" in Italy
and am "Debenham" here. His whole language
and bearing convinces me that he comes here
as an enemy and a spy. And if Mrs. Belassis
once gets a hint as to the true state of the
case, it will be all up with me. I wish I had
never sent Phil away on that voyage.'

'Why so?'

'Because, if I could, I would fetch him back
at all risks. I would tell the whole truth—
show my accounts, get you as a witness as to
my motives, and take my chance of a prosecu-
tion. I have Phil's I O U for a larger sum
than I have yet expended; and although I
have forged his signature, and passed myself
off under a false name, I think I might, by
counsel's aid, get off pretty easily. But I
don't choose to risk it, with Phil out of reach

on the high seas. Things would be more complicated, and disagreeable insinuations might
be cast at me. I wish he had never gone;
but as he has, I must try to hold out these few
months longer, and then, when he is once
back, whether ill or well, he shall come to
Ladywell, and I will abdicate in his favour. I
think I shall have pretty well broken Belassis'
power by that time, and opened the eyes of
the executors. He will never regain the as-
cendency he once had here.'

'Oh yes, you must certainly hold out. I
will help you. I am sure I can hold the
Belassis faction at bay, if I can do no
more. You are certain that Philip Debenham
has sailed?'

'Quite certain. I have received, through
Dr. Schneeberger, a letter from his medical
friend under whose care Phil travels. It was
written on board the vessel, and said that the
journey had been safely accomplished, that
Phil had borne it well, though without any
sign of returning powers, and that they were
to sail before midnight. He will be far enough
away by now.'

'Safely out of Mrs. Belassis' or the Italian's

reach, anyway,' said Miss Marjory. 'I wonder who this Italian can be? A spy of hers?'

'Not possible, I think. He came as a guest to a Mr. Meredith, a sculptor here, with an introduction from a relative of theirs in Florence who has known him for several years. I made, for my own satisfaction, as many close inquiries as I could without attracting attention. He says he knew Philip well, and me slightly; that he met us in Rome and Naples. I dare say it is all true enough—indeed it must be, for he recalls incidents that I remember quite well, only I don't remember him.'

'This is interesting and romantic,' said Miss Marjory, fanning herself gently. 'I will tackle this fascinating Italian, and see if I cannot pluck out the heart of his mystery.'

'I wish you could,' said Tor.

'Does he speak English?'

'No; only Italian and French, so far as I know.'

'Well, well, I am old-fashioned enough to speak Italian. When I was young, it was the fashion to learn only a few things, and those well. Girls were not encouraged then to dabble in science and metaphysics, and play at atheism and agnosticism when they should be practising their scales and learning their catechism. We were not at all learned young ladies in my day. We didn't look down on our parents, sneer at the clergy, or aspire to the "higher culture" and "higher morality," or whatever their new-fangled jargon may be; but we were taught how to behave ourselves in the company of our elders, we did not lounge or yawn when obliged to listen to conversation rather above our heads, nor did we interrupt our betters or interfere whenever we happened to disagree. We did not talk big about universal equality or socialistic philanthropy, but I flatter myself we understood our duty to our neighbour better than this generation understands it. And I venture to say I can talk Italian against any modern young lady extant, however learned she may be.'

Once get Miss Marjory upon any of her pet themes, and she was certain to wax eloquent. Tor was quite content to listen, and the late experiences he had had of nineteenth-century culture inclined him to agree with Miss Marjory's view of the case. Men are proverbially averse to the higher education of women.

'Well, Miss Marjory,' said Tor, 'you will have that opportunity to-night; for I have asked Signor Pagliadini to dine here, and you will be able to tackle him to your heart's content.'

'To dine here!' echoed Miss Marjory. 'Why, I thought you were sworn foes.'

'Not at all; we are nominally on excellent terms. In public he has not said one unpleasant word. It is in a private interview that he was so disagreeable. Whatever his motive is, he does not wish to drive me to strong measures. I believe I shall have fair warning if he makes up his mind to attack me.'

'I will tackle him,' said Miss Marjory, with a certain satisfaction in her tone. 'I flatter myself I shall be able to discover who he is and what he wants.'

Tor was quite of the same opinion. He believed that Miss Marjory could do anything she had a mind to, and was content to hand over Signor Pagliadini to her tender mercies, to be turned inside out, or submitted to any other process that might seem good to her.

' My sister and my aunt do not understand Italian,' he went on to say, ' so that they will not be a bit the wiser for any conversation which they may overhear.'

' Ah, perhaps that is as well,' said Miss Marjory.

Ethel Hardcastle and Maud Debenham had meantime struck up a great friendship, after the manner of young girls. Ethel was always ready to admire and adore anyone who was kind and pretty and good to her ; and anything like a strong will or an originality of disposition struck her as something peculiarly desirable. Thus in a couple of hours' time the young mistress of Ladywell, with her frank gracious ways, her fresh, charming face, and her saucy independent speech, had altogether bewitched the less-favoured but simpleminded Ethel, and Maud became the object of her youthful and generous enthusiasm.

Maud liked to be admired, and therefore she liked Ethel ; and because she liked her, she waxed confidential; and an acute observer of human nature might safely aver that a stage

35—2

had already been arrived at when long con-
versations in one another's rooms at night, of
a peculiarly and almost needlessly confidential
character, would become inevitable.

Tor became aware of this sudden friendship when he arrived in the drawing-room
shortly before the dinner-hour, and found
the two girls deep in talk in a distant
window.

Miss Marjory looked remarkably well—
every inch the gentlewoman she was—in her
rich amber satin and costly lace, which set off
to peculiar advantage her small dark head and
bright animated eyes. She had the distin-
guished, high-bred look which seems growing
more and more rare in these modern times,
and which no amount of outward magnificence
can ever simulate.

' Signor Pagliadini,' announced the servant,
throwing open the door ; and Miss Marjory's
keen eyes were riveted in a moment upon the
stranger's face.

He was presented to the guests, and went
through the ceremony with all the ease of in-
difference. He had certainly no cause to be
interested in these two ladies, whom he had

never seen before, nor was likely to see
again.

Dinner was announced in a few minutes.
Tor gave his arm to Miss Marjory; Mrs.
Lorraine followed with Ethel ; Maud and the
Signor brought up the rear.

'He is very good-looking,' said Miss Marjory softly to her host—'too good-looking to
be dangerous, I think.   Very handsome men
are always rather stupid.'

Tor smiled, and wondered how far this
sweeping statement was true.   He was rather
inclined to accept Miss Marjory's axioms, for
he believed her to be a keen observer of human
nature.

The dinner passed off smoothly.   Conversa-
tions in English, French, and Italian were
carried on promiscuously, English predominat-
ing somewhat, as three out of the four ladies
present much preferred their native tongue as
a medium of communication.

Only once did Miss Marjory address any
low-toned observation to Tor, and that was
when the Italian and Maud were laughing very
much together over some anecdote he had just
related.

Leaning forward slightly, she said in a quiet undertone :

'Whether that man speaks English or not, he understands it as well as you or I.'

'Do you think so?'

'I don't think anything about it. I *know* it.'

Nothing of interest happened when the ladies had left the table. The Signor talked easily and pleasantly of persons and places that both had known, but made no allusion to what had passed between them a few days previously. Tor followed his lead, and was only too glad to be left in peace. Torwood's name was never mentioned between them, and both seemed quite ready to join the ladies, as soon as a decent interval had elapsed.

The Italian was willing enough to take refuge with Miss Marjory as soon as the drawing-room had been reached. Tor could not help fancying that he felt some relief at the presence of strangers, as though he did not feel disposed to show fight that day, and yet had no inclination to become too friendly.

Miss Marjory never knew what it was to want words. English or Italian, it was all the

same to her. She was wont to say of herself
that if she were to be cast away upon a savage
island, she should learn the language in a few
days, so impossible would it be for her to
remain silent.

The Signor seemed pleased by her conversation. Maud had taken Ethel out into the
garden. Tor was talking to Mrs. Lorraine at
the other end of the great room. There was
nobody to hear what passed between these
two, and Miss Marjory could be charmingly
innocent when she chose.

'Have you ever been in England before,
Signor ?'

There was the least possible hesitation
before the answer came.

'As a child, Madame, I was here ; but I
have little recollection of it.'

'Was it this part of the world that you
visited then ?'

He smiled and shook his head.

'That I cannot say. I cannot remember
well enough.'

'You have seen London, of course ?'

'I spent one night there on my way here.
That is all my acquaintance with it.'

'You were in a desperate hurry to reach these remote parts,' remarked Miss Marjory, laughing. 'Most men would not have hastened away quite so fast from the gaieties of a London season.'

'I—I had an introduction to Mr. Meredith,' answered the stranger with a very slight embarrassment of manner, which did not escape Miss Marjory.

'Well, I imagine the introduction would have kept,' she answered lightly. 'I suppose the fact of the case is, that you had paid Homburg or Baden, or Paris perhaps, a long visit first, and had seen enough of the delights of life to satiate you for a time. Or perhaps,' she added slily, 'you were afraid that your reputation would reach this place before you, and scare simple country people, who do not understand gay doings.'

The young man looked relieved at having his way made so plain for him. He bowed and smiled, and remarked with edifying admiration that the Signora was quite too clever —her eyes saw through everything, like the sun at noonday.

'I always did say my eyes saw a little

farther than other people's,' answered Miss
Marjory, with a little laugh. 'What a charming man our host is!' she continued, after a
while. 'So superior to most young men of
the present day—just as his father was before
him; they are remarkably alike.'

'You were acquainted, then, with Mr.
Debenham, our good friend's father?'

'Oh yes; his father and I were great friends.
Like father, like son, you know, Signor. It
is quite so in this case—charming men both.'

Signor Pagliadini looked intently at her
through his glasses. Miss Marjory returned
the glance with the frankest possible ease.

'Think I've puzzled him there,' she remarked to herself. 'If the son is so like the
father, he can hardly rank as an impostor.'

'I did not know Mr.—our friend's father,'
said the Signor slowly. 'He is not at all
like his sister.'

'Do you think not?' returned Miss Marjory,
in her brisk way. 'Well, now, I should have
called them quite as much alike as the average
run of brothers and sisters. He is a little
fairer, and is bronzed, of course, by sun and
wind, but they have the same clear skin and

good colouring, the same kind of open foreheads and well-marked brows ; and a wonderful similarity in disposition, so frank, and pleasant, and unaffected. Oh yes, no one can doubt that there is a strong affinity between them.'

Signor Pagliadini sat silent and absorbed.

'Come, Signor,' recommenced Miss Marjory, after a pause, 'I must not become wearisome on the subject of my old friend's children. The topic cannot be very interesting to you, even though you are a friend also;' and without any effort she shifted the conversation dexterously this way and that, seemingly quite at random, as is natural when two strangers sit down to 'make talk,' but with a method in her apparent aimlessness, of which, however, her interlocutor was quite unconscious.

They parted on the best of terms, and with the mutual hope of future meetings.

'I must have a breath of fresh air before I am an hour older,' said Miss Marjory, drawing a long breath. 'May I step out a few minutes, Mr. Debenham, and look at the stars?'

'We will look at them together,' said Tor; and he gave her his arm, and walked

her off, unheeding Maud's demure look of
congratulation, and gentle pat on the back, as
he passed her. 'Well,' he said, as they stood
together in the warm summer night, 'have
you made out anything?'

'That man is a spy!' she answered with
energy and decision. 'Who and what he is
besides, I have not yet made out; but he is a
spy!'

'I believe it; but what makes you so
certain?'

'I am certain because he has not got his
story right. He is masquerading — pre-
tending to be what he is not, and he is all
confused as to his antecedents. Fancy being
so stupid as to try and play a part without
knowing exactly how to do it, and what to
say—just like a man! Men are such clumsy
creatures! One time he told me he had just
come from Florence, from a Signor Something
who gave him an introduction. Then he
said another time he had been in Rome
until he came here, and had travelled straight
to England; and once he slipped out something which showed he had been in Germany
quite lately; but he saw he had tripped that

time, and tried to explain his words away—
the very stupidest thing he could have done,
of course. He didn't know how many times
he contradicted himself, but I kept count.
Whoever that man is, he is playing a part,
and he is a spy!'

CHAPTER XIII.

PLOTS AND COUNTERPLOTS.

MISS MARJORY was convinced by the experiences gathered in a few hours' time, that Tor's position was growing distinctly awkward, and might easily become dangerous.

Signor Pagliadini was a spy—of that she was fully convinced; though what could be his motive for playing such a part, or who could have set him on to do it, still remained a mystery.

He could hardly be an emissary of Belassis. If that worthy had discovered the imposition practised by Tor, he would not have any need to bring forward a foreigner to expose the fraud. A much simpler and more effective way would be to expose it himself, which could be done, without any great difficulty if once the clue had been secured.

It was improbable to the last degree that a stranger, totally unconcerned in the matter, should give himself all the trouble Signor Pagliadini was now doing, simply from an abstract love of justice; yet, if not a creature of Belassis, nor yet a total stranger, who could this man possibly be?

Miss Marjory was a shrewd woman; and although her quick wits often led her to conclusions for which no logical premises could be adduced, these same conclusions had a remarkable way of turning out right in the end, and therefore she had learned to put a greater confidence in them than circumstances seemed always to warrant.

No stranger, Miss Marjory argued, who had simply known these two Englishmen abroad, would care two straws about the matter, even if he did find out that they had made an exchange of names. He would either think that he had been mistaken the first time as to their identity, or else he would conclude that one was acting for the other, and would never dream of interfering. Englishmen were all more or less mad, he would conclude, and were best let alone.

Signor Pagliadini evidently knew of the existence of the real Phil, and concluded, not unnaturally, that an unfair advantage was being taken of his helplessness. But why he should interest himself in the matter, and take Phil's supposed quarrel upon himself, was a question which was hard to answer, and the only theory she could form was conclusively negatived by Tor.

She suggested to him the doubt, whether it was possible that Philip Debenham had had a momentary return of consciousness, and had gained some vague idea of what was going on. Might he not (feeling himself helpless and in-jured) have believed himself to be a prisoner, and enlisted the aid of some able-bodied friend to go and discover the true state of the case, and do what he could for the absent master, who was being thus defrauded ?

But Tor smiled at such a notion.

Phil and he understood one another far too well for such a doubt to be possible. Eighteen years of close friendship could stand a stronger test than this. If Phil had recovered enough

to realize that Tor had changed their names,
he would understand in a moment that there
was some good reason for such an act, and
would fall into the arrangement with the confiding placidity of his nature. Besides, the
thing was impossible. The German doctor,
who was the simplest-minded of men, had
promised to give Tor immediate warning of
any change in his friend's condition. He and
his sister were the only people who had been
near Phil these three months past, until he had
taken the journey; and he knew for certain
that there had been no return to sensibility.
The whole thing was too improbable to
be seriously discussed. The idea that Phil
could for a moment misunderstand him brought
a smile to Tor's face.

' If you had seen the way the dear boy leaned
on me, copied me, all but worshipped me, for
eighteen years, you would know as well as I
do, that he would be utterly incapable of mis-
trusting me, far less of setting a spy upon
me. It was very absurd of him to make such
a paragon of me ; but he did it, and the tra-
ditions of years are not overset in a few days.
Besides, I saw Phil a fortnight ago, and the

poor fellow was just as senseless as a log. If my voice could not rouse him then, I'm convinced nothing else could do so within the next ten days. By the end of that time he was on the seas. I wish now that he were not.'

So that idea of Miss Marjory's had to be abandoned, and she was puzzled to find a substitute.

However, a puzzle was rather a pleasant form of amusement for Miss Marjory, and she enjoyed the sense of mystery which surrounded her. It was quite a novel form of entertainment.

But perplexity did not stop Miss Marjory from acting. Not a bit of it. She felt perfectly capable of doing a great deal to hinder the machinations of the enemy. If he made himself disagreeable to Tor—well, she would soon contrive to make herself disagreeable to him, and Miss Marjory flattered herself that she could be uncommonly disagreeable when she had a mind to be.

'I can be a perfect ogress when I choose,' she said to herself, with a modest appreciation of her own merits.

If he enlisted the Belassis faction upon his

side, as seemed highly probable, after the private confidence with Mrs. Belasis which Tor had surprised—well, if they too joined in the hue-and-cry, she would very soon silence them. Miss Marjory did not believe Mr. Belassis would dare to be a very warm partizan in a cause which would bring him into antagonism with her; though his wife, who was in all probability ignorant of her husband's early life, would stand in no awe of anyone; but at the same time it could not be a very difficult matter to shut her mouth, and Tor's ally felt quite equal to the occasion.

Why Miss Marjory had so warmly espoused the young man's cause she could hardly have explained to herself.

His own rather romantic solicitude over his friend's interests had brought him into a scrape, which he ought to have foreseen from the first; and it was certainly his own business, not hers, to get himself clear again.

But then, Miss Marjory had known and liked Tor's father, and had taken a fancy to the young man for his father's sake. She had been his first and only confidante as to the part he was playing, and had promised

her help if it should be needed. He certainly
did stand in need of assistance at this juncture,
and she was not going back on her word
now.

Miss Marjory never did things by halves.
Bis dat, qui cito dat, was a favourite motto of
hers, and certainly she had lost no time so far.
She had come as quickly as she could in
response to his appeal ; and now that she
was on the spot, she did not mean to let the
grass grow under her feet.

A long talk with Mrs. Lorraine the following
morning, enlightened her a good deal as to the
Belassis family history; and finding that Aunt
Olive knew already of Mr. Belassis' first marriage, she gave her the whole history, and
frankly stated her opinion of that gentleman.
The gentle little widow seemed to enjoy hearing Miss Marjory's abuse of him, which is a
sad proof of the ingratitude of the world.

Lewis Belassis came to luncheon. He was
hovering a good deal about Maud during these
last days of nominal uncertainty, notwithstand-
ing the rebuff he had received. The birthday
was only four days distant, and the whole family
from Thornton House was to dine at Lady-

well ; and in the evening Maud was to hear her father's will read, and was, if possible, to give her answer. She did not tell anyone what that answer would be, but announced that it was quite ready.

There was one person, however, in whom she confided, and that one was Ethel Hardcastle. Maud's love-affair, or rather the matter between her and Lewis, could not by its very nature be kept a secret. Everybody knew that her choice had to be made, and Ethel was favoured by the information that she meant to refuse her cousin.

For a sudden idea had entered Maud's head. She liked Lewis, though she would not marry him, and she liked Ethel very much ; and it seemed to her that the two were just made for one another. Lewis was sufficiently clever and good-looking to please the fancy of a simple-minded, warm-hearted girl ; and Ethel, with her plump, pink-and-white prettiness and confiding disposition, would be the very wife for him—far more really suitable than Maud herself, who was much too wayward and independent.

Ethel had confided all her history to Maud

almost at the first. Her father was in India,
and had married again; but she and Horace
had inherited their mother's fortune, and had
about three hundred a year each. Miss
Marjory had given them a home for the past
six years, so that much of their money had
accumulated; and Ethel would be a well-
dowered wife for a man of not too ambitious a
mould.

Maud had enlisted Ethel's sympathies on
behalf of Lewis without any difficulty; and
when she saw him, she was duly impressed by
his appearance, and much touched by the
melancholy glances he cast at the merry, hard-
hearted Maud.

Maud, however, was very gracious to him;
and when the luncheon was ended, invited him
to ride with her and Ethel, which proposition
he accepted with alacrity. In fact, the two
ladies between them made themselves so agreeable, that he found it hard to tear himself
away; and when he finally did so, it was on
the understanding that he was to come up the
following morning to play at tennis with them,
Maud having challenged him and Ethel to
play against her, single-handed.

Ethel's artless admiration for Lewis, after his departure, afforded Maud great satisfaction. Ethel secretly wondered how it was that some people were so hard to please, but pulled herself up with the reflection that Maud was of course too lovely and delightful to be easily satisfied, and she could afford to pick and choose.

'I shouldn't be half so fastidious,' she said to herself. 'I'm not pretty or clever, or anything like that; and then no young men ever do come to Whitbury. It is a stupid place.'

Maud talked a great deal of Lewis, and his kindness of heart and various good points, and Ethel listened with avidity.

'I'm getting quite an old matchmaker,' said Maud to herself. 'How ridiculous it seems trying to make over one's cast-off lovers; but I should like Lewis to get a nice wife. I think he likes Ethel, and I'm sure she is taken by him. I can't see why they shouldn't marry and be happy, and then I shall have Lewis off my mind. For I've not been quite easy about the way I've kept him hanging on, though that's less my fault than the force of circumstances.'

Maud's friendliness to Lewis had not passed

unnoticed. Miss Marjory's sharp eyes had at
once detected it, and Mrs. Lorraine had felt a
passing uneasiness, as she observed the gracious
manner her niece had adopted towards the
cousin, whose fate was trembling in the
balance. Tor, if he observed anything, did
not trouble his head much about it. Such
perfect sympathy existed between him and
Maud that he was certain she never meant to
marry Lewis Belassis.

Whilst the riding-party was out, he and
Miss Marjory paid a visit to Michael Meredith. She was anxious to learn from the
blind man all she could about the mysterious
foreigner, and to see for herself what manner
of man this egotist and dreamer was.

Tor had related the story of the sick man's
fancy, and the odd relations that now existed
between him and Roma ; and Miss Marjory
had scolded him for being so foolish and
good-natured, always running into awkward
situations for the sake of other people's
hearts or purses, or what not!

'As if the matter were not complicated
enough without your going and getting into
an entanglement like this! You're just like

your father—very big and strong to look at,
but just as weak really—as weak as—as—
well, as a *man*. I can't say more. Men are
all alike. You think you can get easily out
of this scrape as soon as the real Phil Debenham turns up, do you? How do you know
that? Just as likely as not the girl will have
fallen in love with you by that time. (Now
don't run away with the idea that you're very
fascinating or magnificently handsome, because
you're not—far from it. But you're just
the big, brown, easy-going, cool-handed
sort of creature that the girls of these days
lose their heads about; and this Roma may
go and do the same, and most likely will.)
And then the crotchety old father may, as likely
as not, declare that after all he prefers you to
the true Phil; if he's as mad as he seems, he
isn't a bit to be relied upon. He likes you,
but he may not like your friend; and he
may try to keep you to your word. And
when father and daughter are both hanging round your neck, metaphorically and
literally, and threatening you with broken
hearts and grey hairs, and all the rest of it,
then you will find what a nice mess you have

made of your affairs, and will, I suppose,
expect me to step in and get you clear of
them.'

Tor, who had made one or two ineffectual
attempts to speak during this tirade, gave up
all hope of stemming the torrent, and ended
by laughing heartily.

' Yes, Miss Marjory, that is just what I
shall expect. You have drawn my character,
and I will abide by it. I consider it is my
part to get into as many scrapes as I con-
veniently can, and yours to pull me out again.
Is it agreed ?'

' It is agreed that you are an impudent boy,
as your father was before you. Stop! Look
through those trees there. Who is that with
our friend the spy? If that is this far-famed
Roma, the daughter will give us less trouble
than the father.'

Signor Pagliadini and Roma were sitting
together under the shade of a great beech-
tree. They could only be imperfectly seen
through the network of green leaves that shut
them off from the drive; yet something in
the manner in which they sat, and their
evident absorption in one another, prompted

Miss Marjory's remark, and gave it distinct significance.

'What a good thing!' said Tor. 'Old Meredith likes him very much. And we shall have him to ourselves, too, this afternoon, which is another advantage.'

Michael Meredith was charmed with Miss Marjory, and talked on with extreme affability. It was so seldom that a stranger sought him out, as this guest of Philip's had done, that he hardly knew how to make enough of the occasion.

Signor Pagliadini's name, of course, came up, and Miss Marjory displayed great interest in him. She had been so delighted by his talk the previous evening. Who was he? Was he an old friend of Mr. Meredith's? He seemed so well-bred and well-read a young man, he must be of a good family.

Mr. Meredith confessed that he knew very little of the young man, save that he was an old friend of one of his wife's relatives. He brought an introduction from Signor Mattei, who had spoken of him as a young man of rank and fortune, but beyond that he had no knowledge of his antecedents.

Miss Marjory, secure in her unimpeachable position, could ask a great many questions quite naturally, which would excite suspicion from anyone less generally vivacious and talkative. It seemed only right for her to ask a dozen questions, and make a hundred comments, where other people would have hardly a word to say; and whilst Mr. Meredith was perfectly unconscious of being cross-examined, Miss Marjory had elicited the information that he knew nothing whatever about the mysterious stranger, except what that gentleman chose to tell him.

'As for his introduction,' said she afterwards to Tor, 'we all know what an introduction is worth, when a man has a motive in getting one. I could get an introduction from the man in the moon, I haven't a doubt, if once I made up my mind to have one.'

'I believe you could,' answered Tor.

Whereat Miss Marjory laughed, and told him that he ought to be ashamed of making game of an old woman.

Certainly Tor had a warm partizan in Miss Marjory. Whatever she did, was done with a will; and when she once became interested in any cause, she worked for it heart and soul.

Maud was her next victim. She was not quite sure whether she was good enough for her favourite Tor, and wished to satisfy herself upon the point. For even if not entirely what she should be, she might be moulded to a better frame; and if Tor's mind was made up—if he must have Maud and nobody else—Maud he should have, and Lewis Belassis should be made to go to the wall. Under existing circumstances, she could in no case be allowed to engage herself to her cousin.

Maud liked Miss Marjory, and was quite ready to come and sit by her after dinner, before Tor joined them. Mrs. Lorraine was teaching Ethel some new stitch in crewels.

'So your birthday is just imminent, is it, Maud? You should have let me know earlier, that I might have come provided. However, I dare say I can find something in my dressing-case which will supply the deficiency. We shall see. Old-fashioned things are coming into fashion again, I hear. Have you caught the mania yet?'

'Oh, Miss Marjory, you are too good!' cried Maud, laughing and blushing. 'I think they are perfectly lovely—everyone does now!'

'Ah, well, we must see. Old ornaments or old lace. I wonder if I ought to think of an approaching wedding, too?'

Maud's eyes looked mischievous, her mouth demure. She shook her head gravely.

'Ah, Miss Marjory, you want to make me commit myself. You are just as curious as anybody else, I see. You know I am not bound to give my answer till the 24th.'

'No; and I am not even curious about it. I know already what it will be.'

'Has Ethel——?'

'Ethel has told me nothing. You have told me.'

'What have I told you?'

'That a girl of your nature and your name would look higher than *that*. Philip Debenham's sister will never marry Alfred Belassis.'

Maud laughed again, and came closer to Miss Marjory, laying one hand confidingly in hers, with a pretty, childlike gesture that was half a caress.

'Miss Marjory, you have guessed quite

right. I really couldn't. I have thought of everything a hundred times over, but I can't bring my mind to it. Once I thought I could. A little while back I quite fancied it would come to that; but now that I have seen Phil—oh no! I really couldn't!'

'What has Phil to do with it? Doesn't he approve?'

'Oh, it isn't that! Phil does not interfere. I know he doesn't like the Belassis'; but he is a dear boy, and would not stand in my way, if he thought my happiness depended upon it. But it is since I've known Phil that I've felt as I do.'

'Felt what?'

'Why, what men can be and sometimes are. You see,' she continued naïvely, 'I used to have a very poor opinion of them. You know, Uncle Belassis and Lewis, and old Mr. Meredith, and a cross old great-uncle of ours, were the chief specimens I had seen; and really amongst them, and the few local youths I used to meet at the mild entertainments of the neighbourhood, Lewis ranked quite as a bright and shining light. I used to wonder how it was real live men were so different from

men in books, but I did not believe till he
came that they were really bold and manly,
and—well, like Phil is, you know.'

Miss Marjory smiled.

'So Phil came upon you quite as a revela-
tion?'

'Yes, just that,' answered Maud, with her
bright enthusiasm, which found favour in the
eyes of her listener. 'After I had seen Phil,
and felt what it was to have a brother of
one's very own like him, why, then I couldn't
fancy Lewis any more—I really couldn't.
And I should hate and detest to be made into
a Belassis!'

'My dear,' said Miss Marjory warmly, 'I
think you have judged very wisely. And
after your final decision has been formally
registered, your brother and I must see if we
cannot find you a husband, the very counter-
part of himself.'

Maud laughed, and shook her head.

'You are very clever, Miss Marjory, and
Phil is very good; but I'm afraid, with all
your cleverness and goodness, you'll never
manage that.'

'Don't be too sure,' returned Miss Marjory,

with a very wise, not to say mysterious,
look. 'I have a faculty for managing
anything I have once set my mind upon,
which may surprise you one of these days,
as it has surprised wiser people before
you.'

'You are very like a sphinx, Miss Marjory. Please condescend to tell me some
more, and that more plainly.'

'Well, if you must know, it would not
much surprise me, if, when Mr. Torwood turns
up, you found him almost as much of a paragon
as your pattern and idol, Phil.'

'Mr. Torwood! Oh, Miss Marjory, do you
know him? What is he like? and when is
he coming?'

'What a number of questions at once! You
are as bad as I am, Maud. I don't know when
he is coming back, because nobody can tell
when he will be well again; but I do know
something about him; and his father was a
very old friend of mine. I believe he takes
after his father, from all I hear; and if so,
my advice to you, my dear, is this: don't
engage yourself to Lewis Belassis until you
have seen Torrington Torwood.'

Maud looked hard at Miss Marjory, half smiling, half perplexed.

'I don't quite understand you—you seem in a dreadfully match-making frame of mind. But Phil thinks so very much of your opinion, that he has made me do the same. I will take your advice, Miss Marjory.'

CHAPTER XIV.

AN AGREEABLE DINNER.

MAUD'S birthday had come at last—
the important four-and-twentieth
anniversary, which completed her
long minority.

She had requested that there should be no
great 'fuss' upon the day. She did not want
any festivities set on foot, or a number of
guests to entertain. It would be much more
of a treat to her, she said, to have 'a good
long day with Phil;' and in the evening was
the necessary dinner-party, to which the
Belassis household was invited, which was to
be followed by the reading of Mr. Debenham's
will.'

Maud's decision would be asked at the close,
and it was generally understood that her mind

was made up, although opinions differed as to what was the decision arrived at.

Mr. and Mrs. Belassis were distinctly anxious, now that the final moment had come. They had terrible misgivings as to the validity of the will which they were about to produce, and could not rid themselves of the ghastly notion, that at the last moment their terrible nephew might coolly produce a later document, and demand instant restitution of the trust-money, principal and interest.

Mrs. Belassis was certain that no formal or public search had been made in the library ; but she could have no confidence, until the will was in her own hands, that some evil chance might not discover it to the very people whose knowledge of its existence was most to be deplored.

Increased uneasiness had fallen upon Mrs. Belassis, she hardly knew why, by the knowledge that Miss Marjory Descartes was a guest at Ladywell. Personally she was rather glad of this, for on thinking over the conversation with her husband, she was not entirely satisfied with the explanation he had given her of his connection with Whitbury ; and she looked forward with a mixture of malice and curiosity to the meeting between them, which she would now witness. Yet some instinct warned her that Miss Marjory's visit to her nephew boded them no good ; and she was made additionally uneasy by the hints dropped by her spy, of the long consultations now going on in the house.

But Mrs. Belassis did not give way to dejection. She felt she had a game offensive as well as defensive to play, and she believed that she would find an able supporter in Signor Pagliadini.

' Once let this decision be made, and I shall know how to act,' she said many times to herself. ' If Maud refuses Lewis, then there is no longer any reason to temporize. I shall worm the truth out of that Italian, and then carry open war into the enemy's quarters.'

Mr. Belassis was miserable and anxious, but he was not in his wife's confidence, and he did not know what schemes of vengeance were brewing. He did not know the close proximity of his old friend Miss Marjory Descartes ; had he done so, he would have been tenfold more miserable and cowed. His wife, by a little dexterous management, had contrived that the names of the guests at Ladywell should not be mentioned in his hearing, for she was anxious that the meeting with Miss Marjory should take him unawares ; besides which, she knew he was quite capable of shamming illness, just to escape the en-counter, if it was not to his mind. The more she had thought about his behaviour when first he heard Whitbury named, and the story he had told her of his doings there, the more she grew convinced that she had not been told the whole truth.

Miss Marjory was delighted to think that she should at last be brought face to face with the redoubtable Belassis. She knew all about the theory of the destroyed will, and Mr. Debenham's impoverished fortunes, and was not at all prepared to spare him. Being a woman of a business-like turn, and one who knew a good deal more than Tor did of the ways of the world, she understood better than he had done, how Belassis had managed to possess himself of Mr. Debenham's money, and enrich himself at his client's expense ; and she was inclined to think that a lawsuit against him should be set on foot even now.

Tor, however, did not see where the needful evidence was to come from, as Belassis had had the handling of all the papers ; moreover, that was a question for the real Phil to consider, not for him to settle ; and in this verdict Miss Marjory could not but agree.

' It's a sad pity you are not the real master here,' she said. ' I believe you are twice the man that Phil of yours will turn out to be. It will be too bad if that old scoundrel gets off scot-free. However, I think I can touch him up a little. I shall certainly lay myself out to be agreeable to him. Mind you put me opposite to him at table. I think I can make the time pass very pleasantly for him.'

Tor was mean enough to feel a sort of amused compassion for Miss Marjory's prospective victim.

' You will not let out about the first wife, will you, Miss Marjory?' he said. ' I know he deserves everything you can give him ; but there will be the wife and family at table, and a dinner-party isn't quite——'

' Don't be so dense, Philip Debenham. I

hope I know what to say and what to leave unsaid in a mixed company,' interrupted Miss Marjory sharply. 'Do you suppose I want everyone to be covered with confusion? You are just like a man; you think nothing can be said unless it is regularly set down in black and white. Trust me. I will say nothing which anybody else could take exception to. But I'll just roast Belassis.'

'I believe you will,' returned Tor. 'Well, he's too big a scoundrel to waste pity on. I hand him over to your tender mercies.'

Miss Marjory smiled.

'You and I can enjoy it—and he. Nobody else will understand.' Then, after a pause, she added: 'Is it only a family party? or are any strangers coming?'

'I asked the Merediths, and their guest. I saw the old boy expected to be included in a family gathering. He accepted at once, but now his doctor has forbidden him to come, and Roma remains with him; but that Italian fellow holds to his engagement. Odd, isn't it? —sticking himself into a party where he must know he is not wanted.'

'Odd and significant,' answered Miss Marjory thoughtfully. 'I know that man means mischief.'

'I half think so, too,' assented Tor. 'I have been wondering how I could win him over. He can't have any very powerful motive for making himself disagreeable to me. Do you think if I asked him to spend a few days at Ladywell, it might bring him to a more amiable frame of mind? As a guest in my house, he could hardly plot against me; and if he could be won over, he might speak out, and in the end be taken into our confidence.'

Miss Marjory considered this new idea.

'I think it might do,' she said. 'I should like to see more of him, and make out what manner of man he is. I am not at all satisfied about him; and I don't think it would be a bad move to have him here. We could examine him at our leisure, and, as you say, if he has any feelings at all of honour, he will hardly dare to make insinuations against you, whilst partaking of your hospitality.'

This conversation took place early in the day. Half-past seven was the hour fixed for dinner, and soon after seven the guests began to assemble.

Matilda and Bertha were eager to see Maud's presents, and went into raptures over the costly and elegant trifles which stood upon a table, ' on view.'

Mr. and Mrs. Belassis had brought a handsome dressing-case, as a sort of peace-offering. It was certainly right for Maud to possess it, as it had been her mother's once; but she did not know that, and half shrank from accepting anything so costly from people she liked so little.

Tor did not look quite pleased either ; but Mrs. Lorraine was equal to the occasion. She recognised the old heirloom—for an heirloom it was, although it had been ' done up like new,' in the usual Belassis good taste.

' Our grandmother's dressing-case !' she exclaimed, with a look of pleasure. ' It was your mother's too, dear Maud. I have been wondering how it was that it was not restored to you before. I see now that it was waiting for your majority. Ah, the dear old box! We do not see things like it now. It was such a favourite with your mother, Maud.'

And after hearing this, Maud was able to turn and thank Mr. and Mrs. Belassis for their gift, without any embarrassment.

The party was seated, and rather stiff talk
was passing between the relatives, who had
not met in this friendly fashion for a long
time. Suddenly and quietly the door was
opened, and Miss Marjory entered, her amber
satin, lace, and diamonds giving her an impos-
ing appearance, in spite of her short stature.

Maud thought she looked just like a fairy
godmother, with her yellow dress, bright eyes
and resolute determined manner.

Mrs. Belassis eyed her curiously, not altogether liking the first impression she received.

Mr. Belassis' jaw dropped, and the florid
colour faded slowly from his face.

Tor advanced and introduced the guest to
his aunt and uncle, and Miss Marjory's bow
included the whole party, as she gracefully
subsided into a seat, and looked smilingly at
the wretched Belassis.

' Surely we are not strangers to one another,
Mr. Belassis. I thought the name was too
uncommon to deceive me. A second Alfred
Belassis, a contemporary, would be too remarkable a phenomenon. I hope you are
quite well ?'

' Quite, thank you,' muttered Belassis, feeling delightfully conscious that his wife's eye was upon him.

'You have not visited Whitbury lately, I think?' went on Miss Marjory pleasantly.

'N—no, not lately.'

'I do not think I have seen you since you were quite a young man; still, I am sure I should know you anywhere.'

People were just beginning to wake up to the consciousness that Mr. Belassis was ill at ease, when the dinner was announced.

Signor Pagliadini had come two minutes earlier, and now offered his arm to Miss Marjory. Tor took in Mrs. Belassis, Mr. Belassis paired off with Maud, and gladly remained behind with her till the rest had gone.

'I did not know you knew Miss Marjory Descartes. Is she not delightful?'

'Oh, very!—yes, quite so—delightful! I only knew her a little, and that was ages ago.'

'She seems to remember you very well,' said Maud innocently. 'You must have made a great impression.'

Mr. Belassis coughed and stumbled, as he followed the company downstairs.

Miss Marjory's tongue did good service in making conversation flow freely at table that day. It was an oddly-assorted company, and an effort was needed before the appropriate air of festivity could be attained.

Mr. and Mrs. Belassis distrusted one another, and were at all but open enmity with their hosts. Signor Pagliadini was a stranger, a foreigner, and a supposed spy. Miss Marjory was just the one woman upon earth Belassis most feared to meet. Lewis was awaiting dismissal at Maud's hands in the course of the evening. Almost everyone at table had good cause to fear or distrust some one or more of the company; and with all these conflicting elements, it was not easy to make talk run smoothly.

Miss Marjory, however, was not to be daunted by any such trivial difficulties as these, and Tor backed her up boldly. When the ice was once broken, there was not the same necessity for exertion. People began to talk to their neighbours, and a pleasant hum took the place of the first silence, and grew louder as time went on. Miss Marjory felt at liberty to talk to her neighbours, and to amuse herself, now that she had accomplished her more difficult task.

'You understand English remarkably well, Signor,' she observed suddenly to her partner. 'It is very odd that you do not speak it.'

She spoke in English herself; but his answer was in French.

'Madame flatters me!'

'Stuff and nonsense! I never flatter anybody. Anyone can see by your face that you can understand every word that passes.'

'Pardon, Madame——'

'And what's more,' continued Miss Marjory relentlessly, 'I don't believe you're an Italian at all!'

'Mais, Madame——'

'Now don't be affected, and don't tell me lies. If you don't choose to speak the truth, you'd better keep quiet. I detest mysteries and heroics! Why can't you speak out at once, and say who you are, and what you've come for?'

Signor Pagliadini looked tremendously taken aback by this sudden and most unexpected attack. He was silent, and the little depre-

catory shrug he gave, foreign as it was, produced no impression upon Miss Marjory.

'I believe he's an Englishman,' she said to
herself. 'A foreigner would always have something to say. No Frenchman nor Italian
would be shut up like that, nor take an ac-
cusation so quietly. Who in the world can
he be? Can some family lawyer have got an
inkling of the truth, and have sent a spy into
the camp? I don't believe lawyers out of
novels do things like that. I wonder if the
Belassis party are at the bottom of it? I
begin to think they must be. Well, I will
make it warm for them if they are troublesome.'

With her most agreeable smile, Miss Marjory now looked across at her opposite neighbour.

'Have you never paid Whitbury a visit all
these past thirty years, Mr. Belassis?' she
asked sweetly. 'Surely you cannot have forgotten us so utterly as that? You were so
enthusiastic about the place when you were
there. Have you never been there since?'

'No—in fact—you see, I had very much
to occupy my time;' and he looked at Miss

Marjory with a sort of helpless entreaty, which she was hard-hearted enough to enjoy.

‘You left so suddenly, too, without even making your adieux! There was quite an excitement about your sudden flight and expected return. Nobody dreamed you had gone for good.’

‘There was no particular—reason—why I should return,’ hesitated Belassis, trying to put a bold face upon the matter.’

‘Indeed!’ returned Miss Marjory significantly; ‘I should have thought there was an excellent reason.’

Belassis was silent, and his plate stood before him untouched. What would not that dreadful woman say next? He was ready to wish that the earth would open and swallow him up! The earth, however, as is usual in such cases, showed no disposition to espouse him or his cause.

People had a way of listening when Miss Marjory spoke, and her last observation had been heard by one or two, who seemed idly waiting for what would follow. Miss Marjory was quite equal to the occasion.

‘I fancied, perhaps, you had relatives there,’

she went on carelessly. 'There is a Belassis living in the town, but it may be another family, of course. He is in trade, and doing a good business.'

Mr. Belassis had turned so yellow that even Miss Marjory thought she had gone far enough. Most likely he knew at once to what family that other Belassis belonged, and it was not to be wondered at if the news gave him a new pang of terror.

'Must be another family,' he muttered hoarsely. 'I've no—no—no relations in Yorkshire.'

'No? Ah, then it is a mere coincidence. Hardly likely to be anything more.'

Having wreaked some of her vengeance upon Belassis, Miss Marjory was able to turn her attention to the foreigner, who had now recovered from his momentary confusion.

It was he who opened the conversation, and he seemed inclined to be aggressive.

'Madame has done me the honour to doubt my word. Will Madame tell me her reason? Is it merely because I understand English, although I cannot speak it with any fluency? Surely there are many in a like case.'

'I dare say there are; but I have other reasons for what I said,' answered Miss Marjory boldly, on the 'nothing-venture, nothing-have' principle, going a good deal farther than she had any warrant. 'I know more about you than you think.'

A look of uneasiness flitted across the young man's face, which his bland smile did not disguise.

'Madame is mysterious. May I not hear what it is that you have learned of me?'

'I'm not sure that you may,' answered Miss Marjory, wondering how far she had better go.

'My curiosity is burning,' he went on in a low eager tone. 'Madame is cruel to make accusations which she will not substantiate.'

Miss Marjory looked at him sharply.

'What accusations have I made?'

He hesitated somewhat, and then said:

'You tell me I am not what I seem to be.'

'Well, can you look me in the face, and tell me that you are?'

Signor Pagliadini did not even attempt to do this. He merely said:

' That is a grave charge to bring against a man.'

' If it comes to that,' retorted Miss Marjory boldly, ' I could bring a graver one if I chose.'

' Will you explain farther ?'

' I am not sure that I will ; but I don't mind telling you that you are playing a risky game, and may get yourself into trouble one of these days.'

' How so ?'

He looked so ill at ease that Miss Marjory felt her attempt to frighten him had been unexpectedly successful.

' You have come here bent on mischief ; you know that as well as I do. You won't succeed in what you mean to do, and you stand a good chance of finding yourself in a very unpleasant position.'

He gazed at her with an earnestness and anxiety which told her that her words had produced an impression. She had not chosen them with any special care. Her object had been, if possible, to alarm him, and induce him to keep as quiet as he would on the subject of the secret he had discovered. From the expression his face had assumed, she imagined that her random shaft had struck home.

' He is not very bold,' she thought. ' I must make him nervous.'

' I have not come bent on mischief, Madame,' he answered gravely, but not timidly. ' Madame is in error there. I have come to put right a wrong—that is all—to do justice to the helpless and oppressed. If Madame knew all that I do, she would not speak as she now does.'

' I imagine I know a great deal more than you do, Signor,' answered Miss Marjory severely ; ' and I am sure I know a great deal more than you think. I know pretty well what idea you have got in your head, and it is entirely wrong. My friend and our host, Mr. Philip Debenham, is the soul of honour. You do not and you cannot understand him. I will give you this assurance, and also this warning. Do not attempt to carry out this plan of yours, for you will never be able to do it. Give it up with a good grace whilst there is yet time,

38—2

and do not bring upon yourself the ignominy
of defeat.'

The dark face looked more dark than ever
—more in bewilderment, it seemed, than in
anger.

'Who will defeat me?' he asked slowly.

'I will!' answered Miss Marjory, with all
the reckless daring of her nature.

'You!' he echoed, looking very hard at her.
'Why, what can you do?'

'I can generally do anything I have a mind
to,' answered Miss Marjory significantly.
'You had better not make an enemy of me.'

He still looked hard at her—as if he would
read her very soul.

'And you are a staunch supporter of—of—
our host—of Philip Debenham's?'

'I am,' she answered coolly; 'and I am as
firm a friend as I am an enemy. Any cause
I take up generally prospers.'

Maud's health was now being proposed, and
all private conversation had suddenly to be
suspended ; but when Miss Marjory sailed
away with the other ladies into the drawing-
room, it was with the comfortable assurance

that she had made profitable use of her time, and had given Signor Pagliadini a good scare.

Miss Marjory had enjoyed the dinner-party, if nobody else had.

CHAPTER XV.

MAUD'S DECISION.

WHEN the ladies left the dinner-table for the drawing-room, some of the old constraint seemed to fall upon the party.

It was not easy for anyone bearing the name of Belassis, to be thoroughly comfortable at Ladywell under existing circumstances. Matilda and Bertha were in constant dread of what their mother might say or do next; and she, on her part, was in a state of suppressed restlessness and irritation, which she found very hard to bear.

She had not heard what it was that passed between her husband and Miss Marjory at the dinner-table; but she felt convinced that there was some secret from which she was excluded, and she would gladly have questioned the guest from Whitbury, and elicited from her the desired information.

Miss Marjory, however, had no disposition to be pumped by Mrs. Belassis—no inclination, in fact, for any intercourse whatever with her. If anything occurred which should make it desirable for her to be told of her husband's former marriage, Miss Marjory was quite prepared to make the necessary communication; but then, she would make it after her own fashion, and in her own words : she had no notion of being questioned or cross-examined. She was perfectly aware that Mrs. Belassis was anxious to obtain a few minutes' private conversation, and equally determined not to permit such an interview to take place.

It may, under exceptional circumstances, be possible to catch a weasel asleep; but under no circumstances whatsoever, waking or sleeping, was Miss Marjory to be caught if she did not intend to be.

Mrs. Belassis soon gave up the attempt as hopeless, yet she had not the least idea that her manœuvres had been observed.

It was not long before the gentlemen joined them in the drawing-room. Tor's face was somewhat grave; the Signor looked flushed and indignant. Lewis seemed nervous and preoccupied; Belassis the same, only to a greater extent.

Instructed beforehand by his wife (he did not himself fully understand why), he had started inquiries respecting Mr. Torwood, and Signor Pagliadini had taken up the subject with great zeal, and put the most searching questions to their host.

The two Belassis', father and son, had too much upon their minds to take great interest in what passed, and, indeed, a good deal of it was beyond their power of comprehension; but it was evident that the Italian had become excited, and that the coolness and imperturbability of their host had annoyed him more than a little.

Miss Marjory saw at a glance that something had occurred, and took advantage of a noisy moment to say in a low voice:

'Has anything happened? Has he made himself disagreeable? I thought I had pretty well silenced him.'

Tor could not but smile, as he answered:

'I thought you must have been talking to

him. He seemed as if he had been driven to desperation.'

'Desperate, is he?' questioned Miss Marjory briskly. 'How very amusing! I must certainly see what can be done for him. Mind you ask him here for a few days. I think it is time he was brought under our jurisdiction. I will keep an eye upon him, when once we get him to Ladywell.'

'I will ask him, certainly. Whether he will come, is a different matter.'

'You have not quarrelled, have you?'

'No; but he nearly lost his temper. He does not, I am sure, feel anything but enmity towards me. He may not care to become my guest.'

'And how do you feel?'

'Strange to say, I can't help liking him, though he is so troublesome. I'm sure I have never known him under his present name, but I am equally sure that I have known him and liked him at some time or other, and I can't shake off the old feeling of liking. I suppose he was some old chum of —of—Tor's, you know. When he comes back, I dare say it will be all clear.'

There was no time for private conference now. People were looking impatiently at Tor, as if to suggest that he should institute the needful formalities.

'I think,' said he, speaking generally to the company, 'that we had better adjourn to the library whilst the matter that has brought us together to-day is discussed.'

Then, as there was a general move towards the door, Tor said, turning to the Italian :

'I'm afraid this next half-hour will be but a dull one for you—it is merely some family matter that has to be settled and discussed. No doubt you would rather smoke your cigar upon the terrace. I will join you there as soon as I can.'

'You are very good, but I do not care for solitude and smoke,' answered the Signor. 'If I am not intruding, I should be much more interested by listening to Mademoiselle's decision. I have heard from Miss Meredith what is the nature of this family gathering.'

Tor thought this showed a very fair assurance on the part of a stranger, but there was not time to argue the point now.

'Monsieur must please himself,' he said

coldly; 'but all the conversation will be in English, and it is of a nature which cannot possibly interest a stranger.'

As Miss Marjory was to be present, by her own and Maud's special wish, he could not say that only the family could be admitted; so the Signor, with something like mockery in his smile and bow, followed Tor into the library.

Maud lifted her eyebrows as she saw him enter; but she had rather a liking for the handsome Italian, and was more surprised than annoyed by his appearance.

She was seated in a prominent position in the great room, and looked quite equal to the occasion. A flush was on her cheek, and a light in her eyes which added greatly to her attractions, and Tor looked at her with an admiring pride.

He had never asked her, in so many words, what her decision was going to be; but he knew it nevertheless. He knew she could never have been so proud, so gay, so self-possessed, had she been about to surrender her life and her future into the hands of Lewis Belassis— to sell herself in a loveless marriage!

There was an unbroken silence in the room.

'Uncle Belassis,' said Tor, courteously and coldly, 'I believe it is your place, as executor and legal adviser of our late father, Philip Debenham, and as guardian of my sister during her minority, to read the will now in your possession, and any other documents you may have, which bear upon the present question.'

He pulled forward, and placed at the head of the table, a heavy leather-covered chair, and Mr. Belassis came forward, with all the dignity he could assume, and sat down facing the whole company. He placed his papers upon the table, and tried to cover his nervous embarrassment by a pompous air of importance, which was peculiarly difficult for him to assume in Miss Marjory's presence.

Maud signed to Tor to come and sit beside her. She was quite able to stand alone, but she felt as if her brother was in himself a tower of strength, and she liked to feel him near.

Mr. Belassis unfolded his document, and, after a few preliminary remarks, in which he spoke much of his dearly beloved and honoured friend and brother, Philip Deben-ham, and his most dear niece, towards whom he had always felt like a father, and played, as far as was permitted him, a father's part, he proceeded to read such portion of the late Philip Debenham's will as referred to the in-heritance of his daughter.

Everyone present was perfectly aware of the condition imposed, before the money which had been his wife's could pass to his daughter; but yet, when the words were really read, which willed away two thirds of a large fortune from his own child to his wife's nephew, simply because she might refuse to become his wife, a murmur of mingled dis-trust and indignation seemed to go round the assembled company; and, in the silence that followed, Mrs. Lorraine's quiet voice was dis-tinctly heard, saying with distressful earnest-ness:

'My poor, dear, loving brother never, never could have made such a will! He loved his children too well. He was too noble, too good, too just! Oh, there is something very, very wrong in it all!'

'Silence, Olive ! for shame !' interposed Mrs. Belassis sternly. 'You forget yourself strangely.'

Tor's eyes flashed a look at Mrs. Belassis, which it was perhaps as well for her peace of mind that she did not see. He rose, and crossed over towards where the two sisters were sitting.

'Pardon me, Mrs. Belassis,' he said ; 'but so long as Mrs. Lorraine honours me by her presence in my house, it is my place to shield her from insult. She has full liberty to speak her mind freely on this and all other subjects. No one in the world has the right to bid her be silent, least of all in my house. Aunt Olive, I think Maud would like to have you beside her. Let me give you my arm across the room.'

Mrs. Belassis glared at him with an expression of vindictive malice, not often so openly displayed in polite society.

'You shall rue this bitterly, Philip Debenham !' she hissed, in a whisper which only he and Mrs. Lorraine could hear. 'You shall have good cause to know that I am not to be insulted with impunity.'

Tor smiled and bowed in his haughty careless fashion, and led Mrs. Lorraine away.

All this had passed so rapidly, that people were yet exchanging whispered comments upon the wording of the strange will.

Miss Marjory, of course, had plenty to say, and it was not her custom to whisper.

'It's the most ridiculous will I ever heard in my life!' she exclaimed, with an emphatic gesture of contempt. 'It's positively idiotic! People are very odd, and there's no accounting for tastes; but really this is beyond everything. Philip Debenham, I believe you could get the whole thing upset in a court of law. The man must have been mad when he drew it up. I should dispute it if I were you.'

Mr. and Mrs. Belassis looked pinched and blue, despite the warmness of the evening. The Signor seemed listening with the most profound interest to every word that was spoken.

Maud gave Tor a look of half-impatient entreaty, and he interposed to say to Belassis:

'Have you anything more to add, before my sister registers her decision?'

'I have a letter written by her dear dead father, whom that lady has thought fit——' Here Miss Marjory turned suddenly round and looked him full in the face. The effect was instantaneous. The words died away into silence, and he concluded feebly enough : 'A letter to Maud—from her father. Will you read it, my dear ?'

'I see,' said Tor, 'that it is neither sealed nor fastened. No doubt you are master of its contents. I think it would be better that you should read it to us. Is that your wish, Maud ?'

'Yes,' she answered readily. 'I would rather it was read aloud.'

Belassis had no choice but to obey. Perhaps he did not object to the task. The letter might possibly convince the company that the will did but embody the real wishes of Philip Debenham, senior.

He cleared his throat, and began :

'My dear and only Daughter,'

(' As if papa would ever have begun a letter like that !' breathed Maud indignantly.)

'When this reaches your hand, you will

have been made aware of my dearest wish for
your future—a wish that has been near my
heart for many long years, and which will, I
am convinced, secure at once the happiness
and well-being of your future life. I mean
by this, your marriage with the son of my
dearest and most faithful friend, Alfred Belassis.
I cannot doubt that the son of such a father
will grow up to resemble him; and I feel that
I am doing the best that can be done for your
future, as well as gratifying my own earnest
wish, when I try to do that which will make
you a happy woman for life. When your name
is Belassis I shall not know an ungratified
wish ; and if, as is probable, I shall not live
to see the day on which your choice is made,
you will know that by consenting to a marriage with your cousin, you will be at once
securing to yourself the fortune which I have
conditionally left to you, and doing that
which has been, and always will be, the most
sincere wish of your affectionate father,

' Philip Debenham.'

Dead silence followed the reading of this
elegantly worded epistle.

Philip Debenham had been a man of high culture and refined scholarly tastes. His letters had been models of the art of diction. Anything clumsy in construction, or faulty in expression, had certainly never issued from his pen; and anyone who had ever known him in his lifetime, or had even known what manner of man he was, must be convinced that whether or not that letter was written by himself, its contents had never been composed by him.

The prolonged silence occasioned Belassis a feeling of discomfort he hardly understood. He broke it himself, by turning to Maud with a smile meant to be insinuating and paternal.

' There, my dear girl, you hear now what was the real wish of your dear father. May I hope that his wishes will be carried out by you, and that I shall soon have the happiness of welcoming you as a daughter ?'

Maud's eyes glowed with a strange light. Dim remembrances of her dead father had risen up within her, and she felt a burning indignation against anyone who could so have abused his confidence and exercised so great a power over him.

She rose and spoke with a firmness which

showed that she was actuated by no mere girlish caprice.

'My decision was made long ago, Uncle Belassis ; but even had it not been, what I have now heard would have settled the matter. My father never wrote that letter, except at your dictation. He only made that will under your coercion. I know it as well as possible, in spite of anything you may choose to say. Uncle Belassis, I will never marry your son; and I will never call you uncle again ; you have been a false friend, a cruel guardian, and a dishonest man. I have made my decision, and you hear it now. I will lose the money. I will not marry any son of yours. Philip will take care of me. He will be my guardian as well as my brother now.'

She turned to him with a proud and loving look ; and he stood up beside her, and drew her hand within his arm. It was a quiet but significant gesture, and Maud looked up in his face with a smile.

Then she turned to Lewis, and held out her other hand.

'Lewis,' she said, 'you know I like you. I am sorry I cannot like you better. It is not

your fault that you are a Belassis—you are
not a bit like one ; and I am very sorry for
you. I am glad you will be rich, anyway,
and we will always be friends.'

But the conclave was not over yet. Miss
Marjory's tongue could never be silent in
moments of excitement, and now that she had
held her peace as long as it was possible to
do so, she burst out again.

' It's the most infamous conspiracy I ever
heard of—as clear a case of coercion as ever
was brought into a court of law. Will !
letter ! Stuff and nonsense ! I believe the
whole thing is a great forgery !'

Belassis looked furious ; but he dared not
fly out at Miss Marjory.

' Anybody is welcome to examine them ;
they are absolutely genuine—will and letter
both. Who knows Philip Debenham's handwriting and signature ? I appeal to them.'

But Miss Marjory paid no heed to him.
She had flown back to her former train of
thought.

' Philip Debenham, you must dispute that
will. If there is any equity in law, you can
get it reversed as easily as possible. There

could not be a clearer case of bribery and corruption, or whatever they call it—at least of coercion and fraud. Anyone with half an eye could see exactly how it had all happened. You have as good a case, I should say, as a man could wish. Take counsel's opinion at once, and act accordingly. I should dispute that will to the death, if I were you.'

'There will be no need to do that,' said Lewis, coming forward and speaking for the first time, 'for I decline to take advantage of it. I am convinced, like other people, that there is something odd about that condition. Anyway, it is a very unjust one. When the money comes to me, I shall make it over to Maud. I should be ashamed to live upon her fortune.'

Miss Marjory jumped up, and shook him by the hand.

'Spoken like a man!' she said with approbation. 'You are no Belassis, young man, in spite of your name. I have a great respect for your character from this moment.'

'No—no, Lewis,' interposed Maud. 'The money is yours, and you must have it. I think I am rather glad for you to have something. You must not make it over to me.'

' If you do, you idiot of a boy,' growled Belassis, whose face was purple, ' I'll cut you off with a shilling! I'll turn you out of my house—I'll make a beggar of you before a week is over !'

' I think I'd as soon be a beggar, as loafing round at home doing nothing,' remarked Lewis slowly. 'I dare say if I tried I could get some sort of a berth. I'm not such a fool as I look.'

' I'll help you!' cried Miss Marjory eagerly —' I'll stand your friend. I'll soon find something you can do. I like to see a man who wishes to be independent. Don't be downhearted. Trust to me.'

' And to me,' said Tor, ' if you take a step like that. I'll try to ensure that you never repent it.'

Belassis looked daggers at his son, and would have spoken again, but that his wife, who had crossed the room during the confusion, laid a warning hand upon his arm.

' Say no more now. Lewis is a mere baby; but he is obstinate, and will only commit himself deeper and deeper if you oppose him now. We will soon take the nonsense out of him when we have him alone.'

' He *must* not do it—it would ruin us!' gasped Belassis helplessly.

' He shall not do it. I will take care of it. Now come, don't give way, or play the fool. Quite enough odium and contempt has fallen to our share to-day, without your adding to the burden by your cowardice. We had better get away as fast as we can, or that hateful little yellow woman will be making fresh discoveries.'

' I'm sure I don't want to stay,' groaned her husband, with evident sincerity. ' It's the most awful evening I've ever spent in my life. Let's get up and go. I'll tell them that I'll not stay here to be insulted any longer.'

He tried to assume his dignified air, but was promptly snubbed by his wife.

' You'll do no such thing! You'll just sit there till I make the move! We've had quite enough of your muddling for one evening!'

Mrs. Belassis spoke viciously, because she felt vicious, not because she had any special grudge against her husband at this particular moment.

Her eyes wandered round in search of one face, and when her glance encountered that of Signor Pagliadini, something like a magnetic attraction seemed to draw the two into an isolated corner.

Mrs. Belassis was furious. The last link which bound her to a peaceable policy was now snapped asunder, and she was eager to declare war at all hazards. She was still greatly in the dark as to how the onslaught could be made; but she knew that her nephew could be attacked with advantage in some quarter or other, and that the Italian knew better than she did how to plan the campaign. Desperation gave her boldness.

'Monsieur,' she began, in a vigorous whisper, 'does it not seem to you time to put an end to this game?'

'High time!' he answered gloomily.

'If we do not bestir ourselves,' continued she, feeling her way so as to lead him as far as possible to commit himself, 'things will have got beyond our power. We must not let them go too far.'

A very sombre light glowed in the handsome eyes of the stranger.

' I agree entirely with Madame.'

She looked eagerly at him.

' Are you prepared, then, to act ?'

After a momentary hesitation, he answered :

' I believe I am.'

' And I,' said she, ' will assist you.'

He did not respond warmly to this generous offer; but Mrs. Belassis would not be discouraged.

' Two heads, you know, Monsieur, are better than one !'

' Madame is right.'

' And I am not an ally to be despised. I know much of all the history of the family.'

' True—very true !' he seemed to reflect. ' Perhaps, Madame, we had better meet somewhere soon, where we can discuss this difficult question.'

' To-morrow, then,' she answered eagerly. ' Meet me to-morrow by that fallen tree, where we talked before. At eleven o'clock I will be there. Do not forget.'

' I will not,' he answered.

But this appointment with Mrs. Belassis did not hinder him from accepting with alacrity Tor's invitation to pay a short visit to Ladywell; and two days later was fixed as the date when he might commence his sojourn there.

'That man and Mrs. Belassis,' remarked Miss Marjory, as she watched the departure of the company—'mark my word, that man and Mrs. Belassis mean mischief!'

END OF VOL. II.

BILLING AND SONS, PRINTERS, GUILDFORD.
G., C. & Co.

www.ingramcontent.com/pod-product-compliance
Lightning Source LLC
Chambersburg PA
CBHW060558030726
47498CB00005B/1439